The Day I Found Out Who I Was

Karen Scott

Published in Hampton, VA, by Fruition Publishing Concierge Services. Fruition Publishing Concierge Services is a division of Alesha Brown, LLC.

Fruition Publishing Concierge Services can bring authors to your live event. For more information or to book an event, visit Fruition Publishing Concierge Services at

www.FruitionPublishing.com

ISBN: 978-1-954486-11-9 Paperback

ISBN: 978-1-954486-12-6 eBook

Library of Congress Control Number: 2021912665

Table of Contents

The Reunion

We were waiting for our tab at Olive Garden. I offered to pay because I know how Chris is plus he had me the last time. The waiter had whirled around us several times. The restaurant was busy. A nearby high school had graduation and we were a part of the celebratory rush.

Chris looked over at the to-go counter and noticed a well-dressed black woman in a maroon dress that was cinched in all the right places. Her hair was pulled back in a low bun. She must've worked for the high school because a few of the students greeted her.

"Well isn't she lovely?" Chris said with a lusty grin in her direction.

Our table was near the door and you could hear how well-spoken she was as she placed her order.

"I know her from somewhere," I said.

"Josh, you always know someone from somewhere," Chris mocked.

Spending years in *the life*, you meet different types of people, but that's not something you explain to a co-worker. Generally, if I recognized people, they use to be my customer or I use to be theirs. I had stopped saying that so much because I would be telling people's business including mine.

For some strange reason, I couldn't place her. I studied her face. She felt us staring at her and turned to us and smiled. She quickly did a double-take, turned toward me again and studied my face.

Mary? It couldn't be her. I could not believe what I was seeing. I rose to go speak to her.

"No buddy, I saw her first," Chris said in jest.

But it was like I was in a trance and couldn't hear him. I proceeded to make my way over to Mary.

"Are you okay? Jay? Jay!" He said alarmed. I'm pretty forward with women, but Chris knew this was something else.

"Mary?" I said to her. By the time I had gotten to her, she was standing by the door waiting for her food. As I walked over to her, she melted.

"Lazarus! Lazarus! Is that you?" Mary said. I hugged her but she grabbed me like a long lost sister. When she let me go, she had tears streaming down her face.

"Look at what God can do!" She cupped the sides of my face in her hands. She held my hand and led me outside. We stood there for what seemed liked forever.

"Good to see you looking all good," I said to her.

"You look well yourself," Mary blushed.

"What's going on with you?"

"I'm a child psychologist. I work in the schools but I have my own practice too."

"Oh, so that's why the kids knew you?"

"Boy, I can't go nowhere!" We laughed.

"Talking about me, what's up with you? I never thought I'd see you in a suit."

"It took me a while, but I'm an optometrist."

The floodgates opened. The more she cried the more I cried.

"Now stop; you got me crying." I wiped my eyes swiftly with the palm of my hand, turning away.

"I'm just so happy. People like us don't become optometrists." She was genuinely happy for me.

"Well people like us don't become child psychologists either."

We started running off the names of people who came from *the life*. This one dead and that one locked up. This one got clean and became a Pastor; that one last seen in a soup kitchen. That one still living with they mama and this one got clean and is married with children. Some of our peers made it out; others didn't.

By this time, Chris had paid the bill and walked toward us with Mary's food. Clearly he had paid for hers too and brought it out for her. Chris was smitten with her because his cheap ass don't pay for nothing. He will split a bill to the penny with his obnoxious self.

"Oh man, we lost track of time. Chris, this is Mary. We grew up together," which was true in more ways than one.

"Hi," Chris said.

He liked plump women. Mary was surely his type. With her smooth peanut butter skin and voluptuous build, Mary was everyone's type.

"Hi." Mary definitely read Chris's energy and gave a dry response to cut that shit off.

Chris was not her type. Chris was voluptuous too and was definitely not the catch he use to be. You could tell that pained him.

"So you married, single, got kids?" I asked. I made it easy for Chris because clearly he did not care that she didn't like him.

"I'm divorced with two children. It's been a few years now but he was such a burden. When you come from where we've come from you want that intact home so bad, but I grew up faster than him and he was becoming another one of the kids. I felt like I was drowning. So I said I'm out."

"Funny thing is, all the things I begged him to change, he's done for his new wife."

"Ouch!" I responded.

"Yep."

"So what about you? Are you dating?" Again, I was asking for Chris.

"Yep but dating in your 40s is hard as hell. It's either the geezers or the kids. I can't find no one my age."

I smiled inside. Her next boyfriend was standing right next to me and just a year older than her if she was into white men. It seemed like they all were these days. He kept a picture of a black woman on his desk. I just found out that it was his mother, but to Mary that was a tan white man standing next to me.

I laughed. "Well you have aged well. Them boys looking for a cougar."

"They looking for a sugar mama is what they looking for," she quipped.

"You look like you used to look, just well-rested."

More tears. "Thank you for saying that. I needed that right now."

I reached out to hug her.

"Should I get an Uber back to the office?" Chris asked. "You guys are having a moment."

Chris didn't know what he had walked into, but this was a work lunch and we needed to get back to the office.

Mary ignored him. "So are you married? Kids? I'm sure your handsome self got somebody. I can't believe how clean you are."

I was embarrassed. Damn, was I that bad?

"Just four boys."

"Just four?" She snapped back. I laughed.

"But didn't you have a girl?"

"No."

She pursed her mouth inward like she was holding back information. I tilted my head to the side because now I'm curious.

I found out about my three sons when I came out. I damn near scoured all available records to see if I had anyone else and my spirit didn't tell me I had more like it did with my boys.

Mary cries more tears of joy. "I'm sorry. I've hit that age and I cry about everything. But seeing you is overwhelming. I get so happy when I see one of us make it out. You are a walking miracle."

She turned to Chris. "He's a walking miracle. This ain't nothing but Jesus."

Chris didn't know how to respond but he nodded to save face.

"Ok pretty, we have to get back to work," I said to get the show on the road.

"I'm sorry. Good to see you." More hugs. Mary even hugged Chris.

"Hey, what's your number? Let's stay in contact." I knew good and well that I was gonna hand that number over to Chris.

"Ok," she hesitated. "What was your real name again?"

Chris did a double-take and I could read his mind. *How the hell could two people be having a moment like we were and they didn't even know each other's names?*

"Joshua Taylor."

"Oh yeah, that's right."

"And you're Melissa Gardner, right?" I asked, strongly enunciating her real name. I remembered her name being called for roll call in middle school. She was absent a lot.

We exchanged numbers and we walked her to her car.

"Let's do lunch some time or a play date," Mary suggested.

"Ok."

"I'm serious. Don't flake on me if I invite you out. I got to find out about them kids," she said with a raised eyebrow.

"Oh and if you know anyone our age whose available, let me know." Mary smiled at Chris. She was interested.

Chris blushed like a baby. I was a bit jealous because I thought she was flirting with me.

The Long Ride Back

Chris and I headed back to the office in his car in silence. The office was 15 minutes away. I was grateful to Chris for allowing me to process what just happened.

Mary wasn't the only one who saw someone come back from the grave. The last time I saw her, we were in a soup kitchen together. She was skin and bones yet still pretty as a peach.

I had no more appointments for the afternoon so I just went to the bathroom. It was my time to let the floodgates flow.

Mary looked younger today than she did 20 years ago when she was in *the life*. Sometimes, I forget how far I've come but seeing Mary was a reflection. Clearly we had come a long way.

I must've been too loud with my tears because Jamir came in the bathroom and asked if I was okay. He was the only other black man in our practice. We were not friends but we were friendly.

We had an unwritten rule of having each other's back in the workplace and everyone knew it. We saw each other in a unique way. He handled all the marketing for our group of four optometrists with eight locations in Maryland and Virginia. We were set to rent a new property for our first location in Washington, DC soon. The rent was high but the amount of potential new patients made it worth the investment.

"I'm cool," I said from the large stall farthest from the door. "I'll be out in a second."

Chris came in. How loud was I?

"If you need to take the rest of the afternoon off, you can go. It's

"

close to quitting time anyway. You can at least beat some traffic since you don't have any more appointments."

Never one to turn down the opportunity to leave work, I accepted.

"Yeah I think I'll do that," I said as I came out of the stall after not hearing any noises for a few seconds. I thought they had both left the bathroom, but I found them both standing there when I exited the stall. I regretted opening the stall door. They saw my tear-stained face.

I washed my hands as they stepped back and I saw Chris telling Jamir to leave.

"So what was your real name when you were with Mary? Or is it Melissa?" Chris asked when the door was closed.

"You don't need to know that."

"Come on. Give me something to work with. You could lose your whole career if there's any hint of identity theft."

"I know but it's not what you think."

"So what is it, then? Who the hell is Mary? Or Melissa? Is she an old girlfriend?" He asked quietly but aggressively.

"No," I yelled. "Just drop it, ok?"

I left the bathroom, grabbed my book bag, got my keys and left for the weekend.

Taking It All In

Matthew and Jonathan were home from school by the time I got home. Getting to work on a Friday is a breeze but coming home is always a nightmare. Even after leaving work early, I still got home at my regular time, which was still earlier than usual for a Friday.

"Dad, you okay?" Matthew asked as I walked in the door. Matthew was 20. He was adopted at birth but we hadn't connected until he was seven. I had an unofficial open adoption situation with his family.

"Yeah, I'm fine," I said, about to snap because I had stepped on two toys by the time I got to the banister heading up to my room.

I'm gonna get Jonathan when I see him. I tell him to play in his room. He thinks the whole house is his room. His stuff be everywhere. I don't remember Marcus being this playful at six. I had adopted Marcus at seven out of the foster care system. Marcus was seven going on 21. Marcus had to be taught how to just play and be a kid.

I know I shouldn't fuss because one day Jonathan will be a teenager and he will hibernate in his room like his brothers did. I need to embrace my last little one (that I know of). But damn all these toys. (Forgive me, God, for all this cussin' I be doing.)

"You sure?" I swear Matthew is my shadow. He was adopted at two when I was in *the life* by some wealthy couple. We had an unofficial open adoption situation so he's always been around.

Matthew was upset that I didn't adopt him but the Carters had money and resources and all the things a child needs except his genes. Matthew was able to get into the best of schools and lived a charmed life. I could've never given him that life at 25 when I had just started college. I barely had myself together. I had to adopt Marcus because he was in the foster care system. I was the better option for him but not for Matthew.

Matthew was always jealous of Marcus for having me all to himself. Marcus was jealous of the bronze spoon Matthew didn't realize he had in his mouth. As he gets older and has children, he'll understand why I let him stay with the Carters. He begged me to adopt him and the latter part of his teen years he would come over my house frequently. Matthew was a better son to the Carters when Marcus was around. He visited the Carters often to keep his little brother in check. Marcus and Matthew are very close but they are night and day. A good night and day but perfect opposites nonetheless.

Matthew's mother killed herself taking the pills I sold her. How Matthew even wants to be bothered with me at all knowing what I took from him amazes me. I wouldn't want to spend days at a time with a man who stole my mother from me. That's a level of forgiveness I have yet to achieve but Matthew shows it to me daily. I am so humbled.

Christine, Matthew's adoptive mom, told me early on that I spoil him as a form of apology. I have learned to forgive myself and toughen up on him. Matthew and Marcus are just several months apart.

Marcus's mother was a nice girl when I met her but I didn't realize how slow she was. I don't know if she was slow or if she was too coddled as a child or a combination of both. Listen, I'm an optometrist and I work with a lot of slow people. Anika was never able to get herself out of poverty and is one of those consummate retail workers. I tried to get her a desk job at one of our locations. She was sweet but she couldn't keep it together. As much as she wanted the upgrade, it was apparent she was a fish out of water.

Marcus despises his mother's daftness but he's learned to love her. She's one of those people who can only offer their goodness which is exactly what you need from your mother. However, her slowness explains why she had Marcus and a few of her other children taken from her.

Marcus is making good strides professionally. He's where he needs to be. He regularly makes the Dean's List and has been recommended for a few internships here and there. You can tell he is intimidated by the kids from stable backgrounds at the internships he gets. He tries to play tough guy. I have to remind him that he doesn't need to self-protect anymore. They want him to succeed too. He should make friends with those kids.

That boy loves his father though. I am glad I got him when I did. I can't imagine how much more he would be messed up if I had gotten him as a teenager. He's still eight when it comes to how he interacts with us. He asks me for advice about everything. He's constantly checking to see if I approve of something he does. Sometimes, I feel like he plays dumb to make me more involved in his life even though he should be peeling away from me.

"Yeah, Matthew; I'm good. Jon, come clean up this house. Get these toys up!"

"I'll help," Matthew said.

I can't stand it. Sometimes Matthew is too damn nice. I already know which one of my kids is gonna take care of me when I get old, but he has to toughen up a little more.

"No, Jon needs to get these toys himself."

"Daddy? Daddy? We still going to church right?" Jon asked.

"I don't know, I'm tired. I had a long day."

"I knew it." Matthew and Jon had now followed me into my bedroom.

"I want to go to Kid's Kamp."

This church had a five-star children's ministry. Sometimes I wanted to be a kid and for them to watch me. All kinds of games, toys, activities. Every time the church was open, Kid's Kamp was available. Pastor Davis wanted to limit all excuses for people not to come to church.

Dana, the director, loved children in an uncanny way. She wore her workers and us parents out with the activities she had up her sleeve. We could not keep up. She required a $100 donation in January and July to help with supplies. A hundred dollars was a steal for all the stuff she was doing. If you did not give, your child couldn't participate. The way those kids loved Kids Kamp, them parents found that $100 both times of the year. Parents who were lying about not having it whined to Pastor and he paid for they kids. These same parents always had new clothes, new hair dos, drove nice cars but couldn't come up off no money. Pastor had to stop offering scholarships because everyone had their lips poked out. He only offered scholarships if they were legitimately too poor or had a lot of kids, not the ones being cheap.

Jonathan loved Dana because she looked a lot like his mother, my ex-wife. He'd changed since the divorce, in good and bad ways, but he seemed to be getting over it and settling into his new normal. At any given time, there were a good 30 kids in Kids

Kamp. Jonathan had tons of friends and was Mr. Social Butterfly already. I envied how free he was. I don't ever remember being so free as a child.

Tonight was the first night of our Summer Revival but I wasn't sure if I felt like going. Seeing Melissa wore me out. This was a new church, Revelation Missionary Baptist Church. It had a nice balance of young and old people and lots of kids for Jon to grow up with. Jon drug me out the house because he wanted to see his friends. I was not going to complain about no child of mine wanting to go to church for any reason. So I guess I was going.

Exposed: The Testimony That Started It All

We were late. After I got Jon settled into Kids Kamp, Deacon Brown told me I was on the program. I was trying to figure why I was just finding out that I had to read a scripture when I walked in the door. Someone could've called or texted me all week if I was on the program.

The church was a bit advanced for a Black church but it still had some ghetto ways. I had only been there a year so I was too new to fuss, plus Deacon Brown held my hand through my divorce. He had been divorced several times so he really coached me to get the best deal for Jon and I. I would've lost everything I worked for if he didn't tell me what to do. He didn't just say, *I'm praying for you*. He was a real friend.

Ever since I've been out of *the life*, God allowed me to have great father figures. Deacon Bo was shaping up to be my next dad since my Dad passed. Deacon Brown knew I could never tell him no which is why he probably put me on the program at the last minute.

He was a patient of mine which is how we met. My version of optometry includes iridology. It's East meets West medicine. Some people needed glasses, others needed healing on a deeper level. With my techniques, Deacon Brown was out of glasses in one year. No one in his family ever wore glasses for as long as he could remember, even in their old age. So when his eyes started acting up, I knew something else was going on.

Pastor Nickles whizzed by and said, "He can't do Scripture today. He has another assignment," and went into his office.

"It'll make sense later," he shouted through the door. I rolled my eyes because Pastor always has something up his damn sleeve.

"Watch your mouth," Deacon Brown said, reading me like a book.

"Matthew can do the Scripture," I volunteered.

Matthew had stage fright. I didn't care. He needed the practice.

"Dad, no," Matthew said.

"Okay, that's fine." Deacon Brown knew what I was trying to do.

We heard Praise and Worship getting underway and we all turned to go into the sanctuary. The singing lagged. Tiffany, the Praise and Worship leader, tried to get the people going but people didn't feel like pretending tonight. There was a dryness in the atmosphere.

Business as Usual

Matthew did a great job with the Scripture. He has a wonderful speaking voice. He sounded less nervous which means my plan was working. Deacon Brown made him do a Scripture and prayer. You can tell he was searching for the right words but he did fine. The audience was supportive.

There was a Christian comedian. He had been to our church a few times and he seemed to get better and better each time. He had a huge social media following which is why Pastor chose him. He drew a lot of followers to the service. They didn't stay the whole service sometimes, but many did. They obviously didn't have anything else to do on a Friday night.

For Friday night services, Pastor always tries to do something different which is why I'm trying to figure what I'm supposed to be doing. At one time, he had a puppet show. It was intended for the children but the adults were on the altar repenting by the time the puppet show was done. The kids were on their phones.

This comedian's pants were too tight and you could tell the elders were upset. They had spoken to him once before about his clothes but he said he *forgot*. How far we've come when men need to be told not to wear tight clothes. The comedian wrapped up his set and the service continued. Songs were sung. Offering was raised. Pastor was making some generic announcements. I had zoned out when Matthew said: "Dad, they're calling you on stage."

I looked at him like he was speaking French.

"Go on stage."

I looked up and everyone's eyes were on me.

"Oh, oh. Sorry," I said, scurrying up to the stage while people clapped in support.

What the hell is going on? I thought.

It was the first time I noticed there were two chairs on the stage.

"In our latest series, we've been talking about *Your Story*," Pastor Nickles said as he invited me to sit down in the chair.

I hesitated. I didn't realize I was still standing.

"Would you sit down, Brother Joshua?"

I took a deep breath and sat down. *Oh hell no.* I panicked. These people don't know me. They're not ready for MY story.

I am Brother Joshua to these people. I'm an optometrist and a newly divorced dad who lives in Roseville. That's all they needed to know.

"When I thought of this sermon series, your face kept popping up in my mind," Pastor Knickles began. The crowd was on the edge of their seat.

"To all the guests, we have been spotlighting people's testimonies. Today, we want you to share your testimony."

Here we go. "I'm not sure you want to know who I really am."

"Start from the beginning. Go as far as you feel comfortable."

I stared at him, ready to punch him in his fat face.

"It's okay Dad," Matthew said, reassuringly. That damn Matthew.

He knew what was coming and now, so did I.

Some of the sisters said, "It's alright." Pastor asked for another round of applause.

I sat there frozen. Clearly I was uncomfortable. A familiar voice in the back said: "He don't gotta share if he don't want to."

Marcus had surprised me tonight. He liked Sis. Dana. I could tell he was looking for her because he was shined up with a new haircut. He sauntered in and sat next to Matthew. Matthew was my shadow but Mark was my gut. Feeling the need to apologize for Marcus's outburst, I begin.

"This is ironic. I ran into an old friend of mine and she called me Lazarus."

The crowd knew this would be good.

"Testify."

I knew from this moment on I had reached the point of no return. But if they wanted my testimony, I guess there's no time like the present.

The Unveiling

I sat on the bed alone another day. I had some customers coming but this day was different. I was tired of it all.

How the hell do you get bored of drugs? Where do you go when you get tired of drugs?

My customers were from all walks of life. People come to me to escape. So where does the drug dealer go when he needs to escape? I had avoided the voice in my head long enough. It had finally gotten my attention.

This is not you, the voice always said.

Fuck you, I thought back.

Today, I wiped up. There was no one in my room. I really thought I had sex last night, though I couldn't be sure.

Where did she go? *Hoe.* I checked my products and, sure enough, some were gone. That was my proof. *Bitch.* I didn't even know her name, yet she knew me as Jay.

I needed some sunshine. I had been to jail twice. Nothing teaches you how to appreciate the sunlight like jail. I had a rough idea of what I was going to do today but I wasn't totally sure. It was already 11:37.

"Ya'll got classes?" I asked the young white woman in the college admissions office.

"We're a college," she said with a smile. *This bitch here.*

"Alright, how I start?"

"What do you want to go into?" She asked, clearly annoyed.

"I don't know."

"What are you interested in? Business? Healthcare? Criminal Justice? IT?"

"Business, I guess."

"There's time to decide on a major. There's a few general courses you can take until you decide for sure."

Finally. Damn.

She gave me a pamphlet with courses and majors. It should've been in Chinese because I didn't know where to start.

"When ya'lls next semester start?"

"If we get all your paperwork, you can start this week."

Damn, I didn't want to start that quick.

"What you mean by paperwork?"

"Transcripts and ID."

I knew I was dumb but I did have enough sense to keep records. My grades were always strong. My behavior, not so much.

I graduated from high school but it was Milton Alternative School. *You could go so far if you learned to behave.* I heard that my whole life. I still enjoyed reading every now and then.

I could respond like an educated person about health. I knew I was sharp but I was dumb. I could get through school but not life. School was formulaic but life was a maze.

"Yo, I went to Milton and I been to jail before. Is that gonna be a problem?"

I'd gotten so used to those things being strikes against me, I just learned to put it on the table and take the rejection on the chin. Don't waste my time. Dats how I stayed in *the life*. I couldn't get no job nowhere so I made a job.

I lived in the hood. I could afford more than where I lived but that drew too much attention to me. A 21-year-old black man living in a three-bedroom house that he paid for in cash. Po-po would be on me like shit especially if I had all kinds of people coming in and out. If I'm casual but not too hood, people leave me alone.

This white lady had clearly heard it all before but tried like hell to keep a poker face. She failed because she turned a whole 'nother color. White people can hide everything but their emotions.

"That should be fine. This is a good place to start over," she smiled.

I appreciated that. "I just want to be regular," I said. The ode of every foster kid. Oh to just be fucking normal.

"When can you get your transcripts to me? You can scan them and email me or bring them back up to me?"

Do I look like I got a scanner? "What time you close?"

"5," she said.

It was already 2:30. I thought real hard about coming back up here. I wish I had a scanner. I knew if I didn't get this done today, I would not get it done like the two other times I tried this at other smaller schools.

I knew I needed a transcript. Why my dumb ass leave my stuff? I'm so stupid.

"Okay, I'll be back today. I don't live too far," I said.

"Okay." I'm sure she heard that before too.

"When you come back with your stuff, I'll have you finish up the application," she said.

"Hi Laura."

"Hi. These are the applications I finished reviewing."

"Great job!" Replied a pretty dark-skinned woman I definitely recognized. She recoiled when she saw me.

"How you doing sir?"

We exchanged chit chat like she wasn't one of my regulars. I felt so above these people because they came to me. They needed what I had and were willing to risk their lives for my shit. But she at least had a real fucking job. She could at least fake normal. I barely could do that.

I finally wondered how could a woman so lovely need crack. I sure knew how she got that damn skinny.

"Joshua has to come back with his transcripts for us to process this application," the white woman Laura said. Apparently, she worked for the black woman.

"Wow, that's great." The black lady was a bit too excited.

"But if it's a city school we can access the transcripts ourselves. It would save you a step, sir."

"Oh, I didn't know that," Laura said.

"Hi, I'm Ms. Harris, Head of Admissions," the black lady extended her hand for a handshake. She was quite an actress.

"I'm Jay," I said as I shook her hand.

"Great! Tell us the name of the school, your name, sign the release form and we'll contact the school directly. That way you can finish the application today. You do have your ID on you, right?"

All the other times I tried to apply at other colleges, nobody ever mentioned this.

"Is this a new process?" I asked.

"Yes. The City Community College has a bit more pull with the local school district. It allows us to skip a few steps. Then when you graduate out of our programs you can get with more of the local universities."

Ms. Harris was definitely playing her role. She started helping Laura get into the right system to get my transcripts.

"I went to Milton."

"Okay. Well, you'll need to take a placement test. We have a few sessions this week."

This bitch moving too fast.

"I graduated with a 3.7."

"From Milton?" She asked, staring me dead in my face.

This bitch not that cute no more. I know what she was saying.

"Okay. We got your grades," Laura interjected.

"Finish up your application. You can still make it to financial aid."

These bitches on turbo.

"Damn, I never got that far," I replied. "I been to jail."

Please tell me you won't take me, please, I thought. I'm used to being rejected.

"Ok," she said and nothing else.

"Sign your application," she goaded me on.

"Please take this seriously. When you apply for student loans, you're on the hook whether you finish the class or graduate. If you're not 100 percent onboard, don't do it. We have some free workshops if you want to get your feet wet," Ms. Harris said like I was 12.

"It's cool. I was gonna pay for my classes in cash."

Ms. Harris gulped. "I bet you will."

"Well okay," Ms. Harris continued as she headed towards the door. "Good luck."

"Laura, print out the transcripts and put a hard copy in the file." She turns back towards me.

"Good luck Mr....?" Ms. Harris said with her hand extended to shake my hand again. She was scared that her drug dealer would be at her place of business. I could get her fired.

Then again, I thought, *she could get me sent back to prison.* I had more to lose than she did, I guess.

"Taylor. Joshua Taylor."

"Joshua? That's a strong name." Ms. Harris was a weirdo.

"Laura, let me know if you have any questions. Get him set up for the soonest placement exam."

Turning to me. "You'll be starting school next week," she said, walking out the door.

These bitches.

Ms. Harris had texted me before I got back in my car to go get something to eat.

Stop saying you went to jail. You embarrassed the both of us when you said that. People don't need to know all that shit. I could feel her yelling through the phone. No one can codeswitch like a black woman.

Ok. Whatever number she was using was not the one I had her stored in my phone as. Damn. That was the last time I ever received a text from her again.

Lost a customer.

Back to School: Where the Bottom Dropped Out

I tested in the above-average percentile. I got my scores back that day but they still insisted I go for remedial classes since I had been out of school for three years. I was one of the oldest people taking that damn exam. I should've been above average just like I thought.

I requested my classes during the day so I can get them bitches over with. That had turned out to be a mistake. It was nothing but kids in those classes. I switched in the second week. The night classes had more fucking grown-ups.

I walked into the building and passed the security guard on duty. He made a face. I kept going. *This nigga*, I thought.

"Brother Brian? Brother Brian?" The tall dark-skinned security guard came running towards me. Shit, trouble already.

I mind my own damn business as I walk towards the doorway of my class, hoping this man will shut the hell up. He comes closer. I look around to see who he's running towards.

"Brother Brian?"

"You got the wrong nigga."

He was confused. "You sound like you but it's not you," he said gasping.

"You don't remember me?" He was searching my face for clues. "How old are you, sir?"

"21."

"I'm 29," he says as if I should know.

We both staring at each other. We're the same height.

"Oh my God!" He backs up with a hand over his mouth. "You must be the son."

I laugh.

"Are you teaching the class?" I look like I'm two minutes from death and he's asking me was I the professor.

"You just like your Mama," he said proudly.

" Sir, you must have me mixed up with someone else."

"What?"

"I'm a new student."

"In a remedial class?" He made a face.

"Yes." This nigga's humiliating.

"How's your grandma?"

"Who?"

"You don't even know," he looked so defeated. "I got to tell my parents about this."

I'm still confused. "Ok, I'm gonna get to my seat. You have a nice night, man."

"Ok, I'll see you next week, Little Brian."

"My name is Joshua but you can call me Jay."

"Can't be a black man with a name like Josh," he laughed.

"Joshua? That's not your..." He put his hand to his mouth to keep the words from coming out.

"Ok, I'm Tim." He took a breath and stepped back.

I walked to a seat and wondered what the fuck that was about.

Meanwhile, at the security officer's desk:

Brian Austin! Brian Austin! He looks just like his daddy. I wonder what happened to him.

Remedial classes? His mom was a principal; his dad was a surgeon. He don't belong in no damn remedial classes.

If Brother Brian was a thug, he would be a spitting image of him with his mother's perfect smile. He don't even know who he is, talking about his name is Joshua. Who the fuck named him that? I guess it'll look good on his resume, though.

Brother Brian was the best part of Walker Christian Assembly. The best youth leader ever. What happened Brother Brian? What happened?

I know it has been eight months since I spoke with either of my parents but this can't wait. Although they both use to be assholes, they've softened in the last few years making a relationship with them a bit bearable.

The truth be told, we keep each other at arm's length. Now I realize that they do love me and worry about me more than I know. Tell you the truth, I kind of enjoy it. Well, you know, since I've stopped acting like an ass.

"Mom! Mom, you're not going to believe who I just saw! Call me as soon as y'all get in!"

Hmm, it's 7; they're probably at bible study. Two more hours before my shift is over. Imma going to be damn near asleep when they call but this is too crazy to sleep on.

"Who did you see?" I hate when she asks a question before she says hello.

"Remember Brother Brian Austin? He died when we were kids."

"Yeah."

"I just met his son."

"What?" My Dad asked.

"Dad, he looked just like his dad but 1,000 times rougher. I can't imagine what happened to him."

"I always wondered what happened to that boy," Dad said.

"Dad, I forgot what Brother Brian named him but he said his name was Joshua."

"That's not his name," Mom said.

"I almost told him that but I could tell he had no clue. I couldn't remember what his exact name was but it definitely wasn't no

Joshua." My parents loved drama so I could imagine the looks on their faces.

"Yeah, I have to find his father's obituary. I forgot too," Mom said.

"Invite him over," Dad said.

"What? Invite him over? Dad, I don't think he knows who we are to him. He doesn't even know who he is."

"Are you sure he is Brother Austin's son?"

"Daddy, I thought I saw a ghost. Same height, same complexion but with Sister Tina's smile. I literally ran him down."

"Brother Austin was an only child so that has to be his son," said Mom.

"Something terrible must've happened. Tina's mother took him after the funeral. She lived out of state so we didn't know what happened after that. I feel so bad."

"We don't want to overwhelm him. Ask him some more questions to see what he says. Maybe we can piece everything together before we invite him over," Dad said.

"Ok. I don't work the next day his class is but I'll still come down here so I can talk to him."

"How old is he?" Dad asked.

"21 but Daddy he looks like he's 38. Just bad like he's been through a lot."

"You were about eight when the funeral happened and he was just born then. So that age lines up right," Dad said.

"That's how I knew I had the right person."

"Yeah, just ask him a few questions. We may still have the tape from their wedding and we might have some other videos of him. Invite him over the first day he's available. Sunday night might be fine. What you think Paul?" Mom asked Dad.

"You know I keep everything. Sunday night would be good, Bev."

"Alright, I'll get with him and see if he's down."

"If he doesn't want to come over, just be his friend for a bit until he's ready. If this is what I think this is, his whole life is about to change," Dad's voice went into preacher mode.

"Yup. Ok." I ignored it. "Alright ya'll. Good night."

"It'll be great to see little Brian but I can't wait to see *my* baby."

"Oh Mom, you're such a mom. Can't wait to see you too," my voice broke as I hung up.

I had my parents for 29 years. Little Brian had his for five months and was walking around with a whole new damn name looking like he hadn't bathed in days. The son of a surgeon and he's in some damn remedial class like he can barely read. I felt so ashamed of myself. *Brother Brian, what happened?*

"Lead us to the truth, Brother Brian," I say out loud.

I'm no longer a Christian but I do believe in spirits. *This* was no accident.

"You spit him out Brother Brian," I said out loud and laughed to whoever was listening.

The Invitation

"Hey Jay," Tim said in his street clothes outside of the McClure building right before class.

"Hey Tim," I replied.

Was this nigga waiting on me? I'm trying NOT to sell as much and they still find me. It's so sad how so many people need drugs to get by. But I have to maintain my business to pay for these damn classes.

I walked into the building. He trails me.

"You see that Laker game last night?"

Sports is the universal language of men. We go in for a few good minutes. I have a few minutes to spare before I re-learn this sentence structure shit. They must think us kids from Milton is dumb as shit for them to stick me in this class. But focusing on my assignments helped me not to look for trouble as much.

"What school did you go to?" Tim asked after we were done talking about the game.

"Milton."

"Milton?"

"How you get to Milton. You smart."

How he know? "I was bad as shit. It was either Milton or going back to juvie and I liked pussy too much for that shit."

"Damn, for real? That must've been hard for your grandma."

"I don't have no parents."

"That sound dumb as shit."

"It's the truth. I was in foster care since I was like a year old."

"Here or back in Virginia?"

"Virginia? I've always lived here."

"You sure?" He asked but his voice trailed off. He shook his head.

"What the fuck? Why do you keep saying shit like that? Nigga you don't know me."

"I know your folks."

"I don't even know my folks. Look, I have class in a minute. See ya."

"No, for real. You not from Sacramento, you from Richmond."

"Richmond, CA? I Iived there a few times," I said while remembering one of the better foster mothers who still lived over there. I ate good at her house.

"No, Richmond Virginia."

"Man whatever," I say as I walk away towards my class.

"Here, meet me at this address on Sunday at 5 pm." Tim said, handing me a business card with a handwritten address on the back.

Shit, this house is in the Pocket. Only wealthy people live over there. You could steal from them and the people wouldn't even miss it because they had so much stuff. The business card was for an insurance company.

"I'm not gettin' into no damn pyramid scheme. I'm not selling no damn insurance."

"Nigga, I know you." He said looking me dead in my soul.

"Just be there at 5 on Sunday and shut the hell up. That's my Mom's house so come smelling like soap and not the Earth."

He still trailed me as I walked into the class. A few of the ladies chuckled when he said that. Something must be happening within me because a few weeks ago, he would've had his ugly face rearranged.

"Ok." I was definitely gonna come smelling like Earth now. I was gonna smell like MaryJane and I'll bring some damn liquor to really embarrass him. I may not shower that morning too. His Mom 'bout to really get a visitor.

"How ya parents live in the Pocket and you a damn security guard?" It was my turn to be offensive. A few of the ladies nearby chuckled again. We clearly had gained an audience.

"Time for class, Jay. See you Sunday." I guess I shut that shit down.

"Hey, Dr. Scott."

"Hi Tim! You see that game?"

Dr. Scott was a youngish, high-yellow professor who could pass for heterosexual or homosexual based on what he wore. He was regularly visibly saddened by how far these adults, many with children, were behind in basic reading and writing skills. Tim and

Dr. Scott get going and the men in the class are off to the races. I was silent.

It took a good 10 mins for the men to stop discussing the game. The women, working moms, didn't care and welcomed the distraction. I was over that damn game.

Do I stink? I thought as I kept trying to smell myself.

What the fuck was going on? I kept pacifying myself with liquor but my mind was racing.

I don't know what Sunday will hold so I'm not going. There's no sense is being a sucka. This nigga is just trying to sell me insurance.

Tasha came over and rode me like a damn horse before she got into my stash. I was glad because I didn't have the strength to be much fun even though I needed the company and the relief.

"What's up?" She asked after she finished and showered off. She managed to get fully dressed faster than usual.

"I'm cool. Everything's all good."

We knew each other from group homes. Once we aged out we both went to the corners-her for prostitution and me for drugs. She was pretty enough but she had big titties. That was all I needed. Even though she was a prostitute, she managed to keep her pussy tight like a much younger woman. Tasha was four years older than me. I had fucked women younger than her who were loose, probably from having babies.

The hood. All things beautiful it destroys.

"What's up, Jay?"

"This dude say he know my family."

"What?" She moved over to my side of the bed.

She knew my story. We finally told each other once we were adults. We kept crossing each other in foster homes, then juvie and now out on our own. In foster care, there's an unwritten rule to never tell your story.

I don't know how I got here. I assumed all these stories that maybe my mother dropped me off at a fire station and left cuz she wasn't ready to be a mother. Maybe my father was in prison. Maybe they died. Maybe they were teen parents whose parents told them to get rid of me. I was not a crack baby, though. Crack didn't do anything for me, even when I tried it to see what the hype was about.

You not like the rest of them, my first foster mother said whenever I would act out. *Stop acting like that.*

She never told me what that meant and at four years old I never knew to ask. I figured she said that because I was smarter than the other kids. As far as I was concerned, we all were the same. When she had too many kids of her own, she sent us foster kids back to the state.

"He said he know my family and he wants me to meet him and his family on Sunday."

"You gotta go!" Tasha was a lover, a sister, a business partner and sometimes a mom.

"Maybe he's your brother."

"No," I shook my head. "It can't be true."

"This is an opportunity to...I don't know. Heal? Grow? Get a connection? This is major."

"He gave me this business card." I showed it to her. I had looked at that card a million times since two days ago when Tim gave it to me.

I studied every number. I studied every address. I even called the numbers and hung up.

An older woman answered each time (I assumed a secretary). Beverly was how she introduced herself before a man picked up.

"He's probably gonna sell me insurance."

"I'll go with you," Tasha offered.

"No." My voice broke but I couldn't fool Tasha. She hugged me until I gathered myself.

"I'm not gonna go." *Just great*, I thought to myself. Tim had turned me into a cry baby.

"The worst that can happen is he sells you insurance. The best that could happen is you find out who you are."

"I'm not sure I want to know. He kept calling me Little Brian."

"You want me to go?" She paused looking me dead in my eyes. "What time on Sunday?"

"5 in the Pocket."

"He lives in the Pocket and works where doing what?"

"His parents live in the Pocket. I don't know where he lives. He works at Community where I'm going to school."

"Maybe they're your parents?" Tasha's mind was racing.

"No, that's not what he said," I replied, trying to go over the conversation in my head for the zillionth time.

"How you have parents who live in the Pocket and be a damn security guard for Community? Yeah, maybe you shouldn't trust this dude. People be having a whole stable background and be doing dumb shit."

Tasha was upset for Tim's parents. "Is Tim white or black?"

"Black."

"There's only a few black families over there and he working where?"

Tasha was frustrated. We went to Milton. We was supposed to fuck up. Tim had clearly made a wrong turn.

"I don't know," I say, half-naked. "Maybe he works security on the side."

"Only poor people need to work security *on the side*," she said with air quotes. "How does he look?"

"A long way from Pocket."

"My Lord, there's a story there."

"I'm sure there is. Where's Mary? I haven't seen her in like months now," I ask.

"Worse than before. It's getting really bad. I mean we fucked up but Mary? I don't know if she is gonna make it. Bag of bones, you hear me?"

That really made me sad. Tasha was a prostitute but her system was clean. She stole from my stash to give to her boyfriend. Tasha's mother was a crackhead but Tasha was always smart.

Child Protective Services (CPS) got Tasha out of a crack house at age six. That was the first time her mom slipped up. She knew how to make all kinds of drugs and had seen her share of orgies.

Mary was the looker even as a rail. She made money as a prostitute but not as much as a dancer like Tasha because she was too small for the black strip clubs. She made money in the white strip clubs though, but not as much as the white dancers or even the black dancers at the black clubs.

She was about our age. Mary would barely come to school and, when she did, she was dirty as hell. CPS finally had it with her mother and took her for good when she was in middle school. She's one of the foster kids who came in the system pretty old. Each of her foster fathers raped her. She begged her social worker to send her to a home where there were no men which led to her first stint in juvie. She stole on purpose, on camera, because juvie was safer than the home she was in. She came out and was in group homes until she aged out of the system.

Mary was homeless until she turned to tricking. Sad to say, Tasha took to tricking easy. Mary, on the other hand, was out of her element. She was just doing what she needed to do to eat. I'm surprised Mary isn't a lesbian.

"The last time I saw her she was fine," I said. I don't know how fine someone can look coming to get some crack but she didn't look that bad.

"I don't know what's going on." Tasha paused. "Anyway, ya ass is going on Sunday," she told me.

I chuckled because I knew she was right.

"I don't know. It don't matter. What's done is done."

"Fuck that. I'll be back on Monday. I hope you'll have something wonderful to share with me. And please get your shit together. I don't want to have to do all the work," she teased.

"Go tell Reesy I said hi and tell his girl to stop stealing my shit. Come pay me like a man."

"Fuck you. I got this stash for myself and I didn't steal it. I paid in pussy."

"Get out my house."

And like that Tasha was gone.

For the next few days, that voice said *Go*. I could hear it but nobody else could.

Customers came and went. Night turned to day and day turned to night. As sure as my name is Joshua Taylor I knew I had to go to Pocket.

An Offer Too Good to Refuse

Tasha called me on Saturday and that Sunday morning to remind me about where I needed to be on Sunday at 5. She told me to get a haircut.

"Fuck that," I retorted.

She came over to my house at 2 pm. I wanted to go to the house smelling like the Earth with liquor on my breath but Tasha talked me out of it. I had a little alcohol in the car so I knew I would be fine. She locked me in the bathroom until I took a long ass shower.

The first time I just ran the water and came out with a towel like I had done something. She turned me around, got in the shower and bathed me like I was her child.

"These people have money. Make a good impression."

"I have my own money."

"You tryna get a real job though, right? They can help you so you can really be out of this shit. Isn't that what you want?"

Tasha was the only one of my buddies who supported me going to school. She saw how bored I was in *the life*. I still did my job but I had scaled back a bit. I put on 15 pounds too.

"Please, get out of this shower. You're embarrassing me."

"You gotta wash your ass," she said as she stepped out the shower. Damn, I was worse than thought. I didn't even bathe regularly.

I finished showering. It took me an hour. Tasha had to come and get me out of there.

She already laid out some clothes for me that she bought or stole. There was black pants and a white collared shirt. Some black dress socks and some dress shoes and a solid colored midnight blue tie. Everything but the socks came from the thrift store. Tasha spent her hard earned money babying me.

"I'm not wearing this shit."

Tasha made a pleading look. She wanted this more than I did. I loved her for that.

"You have to make a good impression."

I took a breath and got dressed. She came back in the room once I got finished dressing.

"Oh my God, you look like a real man."

I laughed because I knew what she meant.

"If only you had gotten that haircut."

She was right. I tried to brush it into shape.

"This will have to do."

"Alright, Little Brian. It's 4:30 already. You gotta go," Tasha said.

I slid some benjamins in her hand as we walked out the house together. "Thank You," I said without looking her in her eye.

"It's cool." She drove off in her Maxima, I drove off in my Corolla.

I took my Corolla. It was giving me some noise and I ignored it because I didn't feel like dealing with it. I use to drive the fancy cars when I was younger but the cops smelled me a mile away. If I didn't look like a drug dealer, they wouldn't treat me like a drug dealer, one of my cop customers told me. So I drove sensibly and kept all my car money stashed around my house and in storage.

My house was constantly broken into. My competitors stopped breaking in when they realized they would never find anything but what they already had—drugs. I would feel when a robbery was coming. I would lock up my stash in storage and only leave out enough to keep the robbers happy. They began to realize it was less and less and stop coming around.

Pocket was 20 minutes from South Sacramento if that. The rich and poor living side by side. I lived on one of the nicer blocks. The cops left us alone. It was mostly older people on the block. They minded their business, I minded mine. Sacramento was just starting to heat up. I got close to the area and began looking for the address.

Manicured lawns. Mini-mansions. Double front doors. White gardeners. *How you come from this and make $18 an hour at Community? Tim, what the hell happened?* Is all I could think. I rolled up onto a midsize house in the area. Tim greets me like a long lost friend.

"Who is that shining like new money?"

Tim gets on my damn nerves. "Where is thuggy Little Brian? Little Brian, is that you?" He shakes my hand and thanks me for looking appropriate to meet his mother.

"Shut up, man." Two older people came out of the house. They were clearly Tim's parents. He looked like both of them. His face was a patchwork of their features.

The mom looked like she saw a damn ghost. She was overtaken with emotion. The older man was doing his best to contain himself.

"Hi, Mr. Taylor. We're Reverend Paul and Beverly Walker. Please come in."

This must've been the woman I kept hanging up on. Reverend? No wonder Tim wanted me to smell like soap.

"Call me Mrs. Bev," the Mom said.

They had a spread. The house smelled like Thanksgiving. I hadn't had a home-cooked meal in months. They told me to sit down as we were getting ready to eat. The house was immaculate. There were two living rooms and two bathrooms on the main floor. One dining room with the table fully set.

The little tour of the first floor included a spare room. The kitchen had all the latest furnishings. The patio was fully furnished and the table was decorated as if they were going to have a baby shower. I heard all kinds of voices. I was only expecting Tim and his parents. What the fuck did I walk into? Thank God Tasha got me together. It would have been embarrassing if I had come here in my uniform: t-shirt and jeans and an unwashed ass.

They told me to sit at the head of the table. Two younger versions of Mrs. Beverly—Amber and Vanessa—came into the dining room to greet me. They both were married. Their husbands were there with their kids; Amber was heavily pregnant. Judging by the decorations, she was having a girl. *Tim, what the fuck happened to you?* I thought.

"Little Brian?" Vanessa and Amber said, circling me and giving me a double hug while I was sitting at the table.

"Oh my God! Brother Austin!"

Who the fuck is this Brother Brian Austin? I was terrified just thinking how this was gonna turn out. Whatever they are selling, I am not buying.

Vanessa's husband Daniel was as Carlton Banks as you could get, only taller. He greeted me with a handshake.

Amber's husband Dante was covered in flour. Mrs. Bev definitely put him to use. "Hey man," he said. Clearly they were just here to support their in-laws. There were three kids around us. I wasn't sure who belonged to who even after the introductions. They had them kids dressed like it was Easter Sunday but the adults were all casual.

The table was set for eight adults. They got caught up with one another. Then the interview started.

"So what are you studying at Community?" The Reverend asked.

"Business."

"What type of business would you like to get into?"

"I don't know. I know it's a long shot but I've always been drawn to medical stuff. Maybe I'll switch up to healthcare and do something there. I'm just doing my general classes right now. I got time to figure out my major, my advisor says."

They all got quiet. "Did I say something?" No one said anything.

"I'm trying to get myself together. I'm tired of what I'm doing now. So I take it day by day and hope everything all works out."

"Of course," Mrs. Bev says.

"What do you do now?" Daniel asked. Clearly he hadn't been filled in because the rest of the table told him to hush. I laughed.

"I work."

"Where?" Now I was annoyed.

"Around town."

Everyone was slowing down. We all ate too fast at the beginning and the *itis* was setting in.

Tim was my consummate servant. He made sure my cup of juice was filled up.

"You want anything else?"

"Don't bombard him with questions, yo." He made sure my plate was piled high with whatever I wanted. He made sure I was as comfortable as possible which made me nervous.

Tim was concerned with me. Mrs. Beverly was concerned with Tim. She kept turning the topic on him. "Get some more scalloped potatoes. You done lost a little weight," she'd say. The Reverend told her to sit at the other end of the table before we started. She refused and sat right next to Tim telling Amber to move over because she sat in that chair first.

"I don't know when's the next time I'll see my son again. So I want to enjoy him while he's here," she said. She said it warmly but it definitely was a poke at Tim. He dropped his shoulders when she said it.

The Reverend said, "Mmm-Hmm," quietly.

Clearly, I wasn't the only guest. Tim had no clue how fucking lucky he was. You could tell he put his parents through the ringer.

"How's the job?" She'd start when she could.

"Beale has some security positions out there. They start at $27/hour full benefits. With your experience you could probably negotiate for more."

"I'm surprised Janet didn't come. Is she okay?"

He responded politely but you could tell he was annoyed. I knew he probably woulda fussed if I wasn't there. Tim did work full-time for Community. It was not his job on the side. They'd given him a raise as he was a manager of the night shift security guards. He assigned shifts, managed payroll, handled employee issues and still had a shift of his own. Clearly he wasn't making that much because that $27/hour piqued his interest.

I could see how Tim could be a good manager. You could tell he was a nice person. Testy but orderly. He managed 10 people. The school had a few break-ins over summer break so he was interviewing for new staff too. They were considering him for the day shift management team because he was doing a good job in his management role.

Beale was a giant Air Force Base in the middle of nowhere. I had a few customers from there. Some Army and Air Force people but some were more of the white-collar customers who only wanted pills. So I knew they had some desk jobs there. I had considered joining the military but I went to Milton. Who the fuck was I kidding? Mrs. Bev said the job at Beale would be just scanning people's fingerprints, making security badges and investigating any security complaints.

Seemed to me Mrs. Bev really liked Janet which is saying a lot for a mom. Janet was an on again off again girlfriend. She was in school to become a dentist. Damn Tim. You a security guard and you messing up a relationship with a future dentist. Now I, like Tasha, was mad for his parents. He fucking up all his blessings.

Janet babysat for rich kids during the summer to earn extra money before her classes started back up. Her family, the Davis' lived in Elk Grove, a suburb of Sacramento. Not nearly as rich as Pocket but stable and safe. She had one more year to go.

"I'm not ready to be tied down," Tim said.

"I agree," Reverend Walker said. "Bev chill."

"I just asked how she was doing." From what Mrs. Bev explained, Janet had a very bright personality when Tim and her first dated.

You don't see that in a lot of black women. You could tell she had a good childhood. She was an excellent babysitter because she would take her kids to all the places she went to as a child. Festivals, museums, picnics in the kids' backyard. Some of her kids' reading advanced when Janet took them on as she had all kinds of learning games.

"She would be better suited as a teacher. I don't know why she'd bother with being a damn dentist. She'd be a perfect mother, though." Mrs. Bev said, looking in Tim's direction.

"Her light seemed to dim over the years. I don't know what happened." Mrs. Bev said, an obvious dig at Tim.

"Mom," Amber quipped. "This is why he don't come around," she said quietly but loud enough for the table to hear.

"Excuse me, little girl," Mrs. Bev said.

"Can I use the restroom?"

"Yeah," the men said in unison. I chuckled inside. It was about to be World War III up in here. I rose to go to the bathroom. They rose to start clearing plates. *I should offer to wash the dishes before I leave,* I thought. Ms. Barbara, one of the better foster mothers I had, always offered to clean up when we went to people's houses.

Just start helping. Don't even ask. They will appreciate the help and remember you. That was also her way of getting more food to-go that the hosts may have hidden from their other guests. Ms. Barbara didn't play about manners.

I went into the half bathroom that Tim directed me too. I took a whiz. I could tell he was still outside the door. Probably making sure I didn't steal nothing. He smart. He led me into the main living room filled with plants and pictures and knick-knacks.

No one even touched the deserts. Our bellies were full. Pregnant Amber wasn't the only one waddling around taking breaths every few steps.

Here comes the sales pitch, I think. The son-in-laws were outside with their kids. It was Paul and Beverly Walker sitting in the solo couches directly across from each other. Tim and I sat on the main three-seater pastel green couch. This house looked like it was ripped out of a damn magazine. There was a nice sized TV right in the center of the room.

Mrs. Bev set out glasses of juice on coasters with a full pitcher in the center. She and the Reverend had to be in their 60s or older. No younger woman would bother to host as well as Mrs. Bev.

As I went to take my seat, I saw Vanessa and Amber who were behind the main couch on some small upholstered accent stools. They were holding hands like they were bracing themselves for something.

The room was quiet. There was a stack of VHS tapes on the coffee table in front of us. Photo albums too and a few loose photos pushed into the albums. No one used VHS tapes anymore. Everything was on DVD. The room was filled with anticipation.

"Tim, go get those boxes of tissues I bought," Mrs. Beverly said.

"Ok," Tim said.

The phone rang.

Dan stood with his back to the door to keep the kids from running back into the house. He kept peeking behind himself to make sure everything was okay on the inside. The kids were oblivious. They was playing with they daddies and with one another. Cousin love. *Tim, let me borrow your family.*

Vanessa went to grab the phone off the wall. "Hello?" Vanessa said. She kept going.

"Joshua? Nobody here named Joshua. You must have the wrong number."

Tim sprinted for the phone. Vanessa and Amber still thought my name was Brian. He had not filled them in.

"Joshua is his name. He right there."

"Right where? His name ain't no Joshua," Vanessa said. She didn't understand. *Here we go,* I thought.

"Ma'am? Yes, Joshua's here," Tim said into the phone. "Who's this?" He asked and paused.

"LaTasha Robinson?" Tasha was in mommy mode.

"A friend of Joshua? Ok."

"Yes, we just had dinner. He gained about five lbs. tonight," Tim replied, laughing.

"Yes, he's fine. No, we're not going to sell him insurance," Tim chuckled.

"Yes we'll make sure he gets home safe. He'll probably be leaving in about an hour. Does he have a curfew?"

What was Tasha saying to him?

"Yes, Ma'am. He'll be home in no time. I'll tell him to call you when he gets home." Tim let out a final laugh.

"Ok. Bye Bye."

Tim and Vanessa came back in the room.

"Joshua?" Vanessa called.

"That's me," I replied, raising my hand as if I was in school. She looked over at Amber like *ain't this a bitch.*

Tim barreled back into the living room. "That woman sounded awfully familiar," he said.

Tim was probably a customer of Tasha's. They could never know who each other was. How you got a Janet and fucking with a damn Tasha? I could slap the black off of him.

"That was your friend LaTasha. She was checking to make sure you made it. She said to call her when you get home."

"Thanks." They didn't need to know how I knew her.

"That's a nice friend who would check on you like that," Mrs. Bev said. "Is she pretty?"

"Mom!" Tim said.

"My mother was a matchmaker in her previous life. Excuse her."

I laughed. I already knew I loved Mrs. Bev.

"Ok. Let's get started on why we're here. Shall we pray first?" Tim took this seriously.

"Yes son," his father agreed. "Pray."

Tim said a short and sweet prayer, then he began.

True Identity

"Your name is not Joshua Taylor." He was fidgety as if he didn't know how to go on. Mrs. Bev was already on tissue number one.

"We want to show you a few videos and then we'll talk about it. I think they'll explain a lot."

Reverend turned the TV on. Amber had to show him how to get the tape deck set up. The first VHS began.

I saw myself in a white tux. I was clean. I was happy. I looked about 30 though, maybe 35. I was waiting for my bride. She was pretty. Some man who looked like her walked her down the aisle.

Even though the video was grainy, you could tell these people had money. A 40ish Reverend Walker stood in the center and he performed the wedding. A very young Tim stood near the men as the ring bearer.

"What's going on?" I asked. I sank deeper into the couch but I could feel my body rise. My ears started ringing.

The next video was a baby shower. That same woman was pregnant. Mrs. Bev was scurrying around with the food, helping with the gifts, still tidying up the blue decorations. Then I came into the camera and started speaking.

I was so happy to be having a son. I was eloquent. I quoted Scripture. The women in the room ate it up. I was so handsome. I looked like I never had to take an Advil a day in my life. I glowed.

This woman's mother sat near her beaming with pride. Her only child was having a son. A dark-skinned pudgy woman who kept saying Brian was the life of the party. I called her *Mom*. She was Mrs. Bev's age.

The two mothers seemed to keep one-upping each other in gifts for the new mom.

"I bought the stroller," one would say.

"I bought the crib and rocking chair at the house," the other would say. This was both sides of the family's first grandchild.

"He'll be a Junior but we'll call him BJ or Little Brian," I said. The guests laughed.

"Tina, what you think?"

"If you say so," she said with an eye roll. She had on a T-shirt that said *Howard U* with a pink leaf with green lettering that spelled out *AKA* in the right-hand corner. Even though she went to college, you could tell she had some hood in her. Even her Mom had blonde streaks in her hair. I had a teacher, Ms. Butler, who had that same shirt. I was her favorite but she made remarks to my foster mother, Ms. Shirley.

"Are we sure that's his name?" Ms. Shirley thought she was dumb to be a teacher.

"You're not like them," she said to me. "Stop being bad."

"You're better than this," she'd say.

Wait. Wait. Was that Ms. Butler in the video? I squinted.

She would do pop-ups at Ms. Shirley's house. Ms. Shirley reported her to the Principal for harassment because Shirley did spank us. She didn't want to get in trouble again so Ms. Butler stopped coming around.

Ms. Butler made sure I was in every extracurricular club imaginable. I just wanted to go home so I fought it. I *was* like them. My social worker said Ms. Butler had been requesting files on me. She was even interested in adopting me.

"I know your mother," she said one day.

"Bitch, you got the wrong nigga," I responded. Even at eight, I knew I had no damn fucking parents. *I dropped out the fucking sky,* I told people. I probably came up from hell. That would make more sense why I was drawn to my occupation.

Ms. Shirley dressed us in the same clothes every week to keep costs down. Mrs. Butler bought me new clothes. Ms. Shirley was offended but I appreciated them. When Ms. Shirley saw how happy I was with my Mickey Mouse clothes, (which I had to share with her other foster kids), she let me have them. Eventually, she just added those clothes to our rotation.

Such a fucking bitch. Those were *my* clothes. Every few months, Ms. Butler had new clothes for me, even when I was out of her class. *Keep him Lord,* she'd pray every now and then. She was a weirdo. Maybe Ms. Shirley was right.

"Ms. Butler? That's my 3rd grade teacher!" I exclaimed.

"You know Leah?" Reverend asked.

"I guess but her name's not Leah, it's Ms. Butler," I said, doing what everyone does to teachers—forget that they have first names.

"She lives in Seattle with her new man. She's a principal now," the Reverend said.

"Do you see anyone else in this video that you recognize? Is there anything else you like to talk about?" Tim was annoyed. I identified the wrong person.

Fuck you, I thought. I stiffened and turned back to the video. Tim got up and turned off the TV.

"Let's try something else." He opened the first album. He sprawled the loose pictures all over the table.

The kids were upstairs now. All the adults were now in the living room. Dan, Vanessa's husband, sat Indian style on the floor taking everything in. *Who said men don't love drama?* Amber and Vanessa had moved up to where the main furniture was. They sat on the arms of their parents' chairs waiting for me to get it. Dante had sat on the couch with Tim and me, eating a slice of apple pie. The three kids upstairs sounded like ten.

There was a picture of the baby being born. Tina had gained at least 20 pounds between the baby shower and the delivery. I was crying. I was so proud of my son.

There was a picture of me graduating from medical school with people around me. There was a picture of Reverend Walker blessing this baby. Then I saw it.

The newspaper clipping. A lot of these pictures of me had a lot of the same faces around me. The people celebrated all of my milestones. And then I saw it.

Three funerals in one day grips the city was the headline. I stood up and reached for it. Everyone flinched.

There were two white caskets lying side by side. Flowers of every size and shape flanked the stage. There was a picture of Reverend Walker preaching. There had been a drunk driving accident. The writer said in so many words that I was the one drunk.

These two people were both only children the article read. He was a newly minted surgeon at 35. She was already a principal at aged 32. A Howard University flag was included on the pulpit.

She was pregnant at the time of the accident. No one seemed to know that though. Three people dead in one night. Everyone in the other cars survived but had injuries. Nothing major but still injured none the less.

My hands shook. I couldn't put the paper back down. I didn't know I was crying until the tear splattered on the paper.

I did have parents. I came from real decent people. I had grandparents. Why didn't they adopt me?

I remembered my foster mother, Ms. Abilene, saying: *You're different from them.* I was already in California by then.

"How the hell did I get to California?"

"Tina, your mother is from the Bay. Her mother took you when they passed," the Reverend explained.

"Somehow, the grief overwhelmed her and she couldn't take care of you. Somehow, you got into the hands of the state. By the time they fully had you she was in St. Johns. She lost everything."

St. Johns is a notorious mental institution in the Bay. It's come a long way in recent years but when someone was admitted there, it was pretty serious.

I kept looking at the two caskets. I looked at it for I don't know how long. Tim told me to sit down. I was stuck.

They were saying things but I didn't hear them. Reverend said something about *records, no birth certificate, they had to rename you, records based in Virginia* and *ward of the state.*

I sank back into the couch.

I heard Mrs. Bev say, "Dan, get him some water. Baby, can you hear me?"

"Jay!" Tim, Vanessa and Amber kept saying my name. I wanted to say something but I didn't know what to say. I kept seeing everyone in double. They gave me some water but I couldn't see. My head rolled back. I drunk some Henney before I got here but this was not liquor.

"I'm fine," I finally said. I felt my bladder release.

Dante jumped up. "Ah, he peed." I thought he was talking about Tim. My eyes kept blinking but I couldn't see anything. I tried to mouth words but they wouldn't come out. I started to get up and go to my car. I was in no shape to drive but I knew I had to leave.

"5150," Amber, the nurse said.

Something in me rose up. "No!" I roared at her, ready to charge. Dante blocked me.

"Nigga you can get it too." I yelled and started to throw punches. He was too fast. I kept punching the air.

I walked away like a drunk, barely seeing anything. I knocked shit over. I just had to get out of there.

I couldn't get those caskets out of my mind. White caskets. They were so beautiful. They were so pretty. How does the death of two non-famous black people in their 30s take up so much space in a white newspaper?

There was so much more I didn't understand. But those caskets. I'd seen quite a few caskets in my life. I thought I was numb to death but I guess I wasn't.

I heard someone say, "911, we need an ambulance now." Oh hell no. I didn't need to be in the system. The cops would find me but, suddenly, I didn't have control over my limbs.

"We think it's a 5150. His body is fine but he's going crazy." The voice sounded like Vanessa's.

"Don't say that," Mrs. Bev chided Amber. "Kids, go back upstairs," she demanded. I heard a little girl screaming.

"Go in ya'll room and shut the door. Somebody will be up in there in a minute."

How many rooms did they have in this damn house?

I also heard someone calling Tasha. I began to cry.

"He's having a breakdown. He got some bad news. Calm down, please."

Tasha would be so disappointed in me. I messed this all up. I felt Dante and Dan sitting on my back, holding me down. Dan had my keys.

I heard a rush in. I heard sirens. There had to be several cop cars outside. I knew I needed to straighten up. I couldn't go back to jail. My next stop was fucking prison.

I cried some more. My black ass caused these cops to come to one of the few black homes in the neighborhood. I cried for the Walkers. I wanted to respond like a man but I just cried for the whole world.

An ambulance AND a fire truck showed up. South Sac could never get a response like this, even during a damn drive by. A medical emergency in the Pocket got this much attention? I couldn't stop crying about everything.

"Sir! Sir! Look at me! What's your name? Do you know where you are?"

Lights Out

"Joshua?" Someone in a nurse's outfit was trying to wake me.

"Back up. Go," the nurse said, talking to someone else.

"Here's your dinner. At least drink some water."

I was out of it. I woke up. I saw Wednesday on the chalkboard in front of me.

Wednesday? What the hell happened to Monday and Tuesday? I stretched out my hand like I do every day to see if anyone was there. I was not in my queen-sized bed. My arm sank to the floor. I struggled to get my eyes open.

"He cool. He don't want no more," a deep voice said. He shook me. "Wake up, man."

I sat up slowly. I had no clue where I was.

"Raheem, go," a woman said.

"Let me have his food."

"There's snacks in the community room. This is for him."

Snacks? I thought. *Community room?*

I kept seeing the same people pacing back and forth outside our room. Some screaming. Some talking to themselves. *They crazy as sh*it, I thought. I was afraid to ask where I was.

"I need you to try and eat some food today. You didn't have much yesterday."

I don't remember anything since Sunday when Dan was sitting on my back like I was a park bench.

I picked up the spork and started eating the bland spaghetti. One slow bite at a time. The Asian nurse seemed to be so proud of me. Asians have some strong damn features. I tried to place her ethnicity. She was Asian to me but she was darker than the regular Asian. I don't know; they all look alike. I guess they're supposed to look like each other.

Raheem was visibly upset I was eating my food. He was very light-skinned and big as a bear with mid-back uniformed dreads. He looked and acted like a lion. He gave off a vibe that he was mixed, but with a name like Raheem, his mother was definitely black. He stormed into the chaotic hallway.

"Would you like to make a call after your dinner?" The nurse asked. I had no one to call. I was always alone. That never saddened me. It was just a matter of fact at this point.

"A Ms. Robinson has called twice since you were admitted. Call her. Tim Walker has come every day but you were under for the past few days. He just left."

I've been trying to get myself together for a month and I already had more people helping me than I had in my whole life.

"No, that's alright." Tasha and Tim will get over it if I don't call.

"Ma'am, where am I?" I ask.

"The Belmont Center."

"This nigga don't even know where the fuck he is," Raheem barked.

"Watch your mouth, Raheem!" The nurse chided. The troublemaker was back. He looked older than me. He might've been a customer. He looks familiar.

"What's the Belmont Center?" I asked.

"It's a psychiatric treatment center. You'll be released when we think you're not a danger to yourself or others," she bent down, speaking to me as if I was seven.

"It's a nut-house. You in this bitch," Raheem said.

"Raheem, go down the hall!" She yelled and waited until he was far enough away for her to talk to me like a seven-year old again. A peanut butter colored black woman kept passing the doorway. She was young, I think. She looked like everyone else in these blue paper thin scrubs.

"You had a lot of stuff in your system. Tim told us you got some news though that caused you to have a breakdown. Do you remember that?" She asked.

I shook my head. "No."

"You don't remember falling down and crying and swinging at the officers? You don't remember trying to run up Mr. Walkers' steps?"

"No, I never ran up the stairs of their house," I said as if she was the confused one.

"What's the last thing you remember?"

I paused. "The caskets," I said in a soupy voice. I went back to wailing.

"The caskets!"

The Asian lady was mad at herself for winding me back up and tried to console me. She kept telling me to calm down. That night, I started pacing up and down the hallway. The nurses' station near me was full of activity even at night.

I wasn't the only one walking the floor speaking incoherently not making any sense. There were four of us pacing. We were out of our minds but we never bumped into one another.

I learned later that I was pacing all of Monday and Tuesday. They sedated me but the memory of those caskets kept unraveling me. The flashbacks came.

You're not like them.

Are you sure you aren't related to the Austins of Virginia?

You're so smart!

He loves any game about the body. He could be a doctor if he wasn't so damn bad.

He never had drugs in his system. He just bad as shit.

He's going to be a heartbreaker. Look at those perfect teeth.

His brain is normal. He's just been through a lot. I remember a pediatrician said this after Ms. Lacreasha had me screened. She genuinely thought there was something physiological going on. For one of the younger foster mothers, she cared the most. Even when teachers had begged her to put me on Ritalin, she refused.

"He's too smart for Ritalin. It would destroy him. Aren't

ya'll professionals?"

The voice said, *Stop fucking up.* I decided to be a better student that year in 5th grade. I needed to prove Ms. Lacreasha right. I had so much catching up to do. In a year, the teachers saw what Ms. Lacreasha saw. She looked so much happier once I behaved.

I graduated from middle school with a 3.5. The whole school stood up when I walked across that stage. Everyone knew I had come a long way. Ms. Lacreasha got a promotion in Dallas and turned me back over to the state.

My father was so handsome. My mother was so pretty. They were so accomplished. Are their parents still alive? Do I have grandparents? I mean are they alive?

I don't have parents, was what I always said to people. Normal people scoffed at me. The kids in the group homes knew what I meant though. My parents must've been 10 years younger than the Walkers. My mind was racing. Another dark Asian nurse came towards me with a needle bigger than her.

I didn't wake up until Friday morning. I found a tray of food at my bedside. Eggs, bacon, sausage and orange juice. I slid myself up and began to eat.

A white nurse showed up. She opened the windows and damn near blinded me. When I finally got a good look at her, I recognized her. A customer. She tightened up but played her position as Raheem came bumbling into the room.

"Mr. Taylor, it's nice to meet you. I'll be your nurse for the weekend."

"Ok."

"You don't have to rush but I have one assignment for you today."

"Ok," I said, still eating.

"We got you some new clothes." She paused. "Raheem, can you give us a minute?"

"No." I couldn't stand Raheem.

"Raheem," she said as if the word *go* was in her voice. He left. He was in his right mind but was just an asshole.

She stepped forward. "We need you to take a shower."

I paused. "Ok." I was grateful she told Raheem to get out.

"Just so you know, the more you cooperate around here the faster you can go home."

"Cooperate?"

"Yes. Go to the cafeteria with the group."

I didn't know we could walk to a cafeteria. I thought they served food every day.

"Participate in the activities we have in the community hall. Take your medications. Go down to the rec room with the rest of the guests. Talk to your caseworker."

I didn't realize I had to prove anything to anybody. I had to *perform* to get out? I wasn't in prison but this sure sounded similar.

"What day is it?"

"Friday."

"Yesterday was Wednesday, though," I said like she was the patient.

She didn't respond. She could tell I was gonna need a couple more days.

I had been here from Sunday to Friday. I lost a week of classes and money. I'm sure I had been robbed. All that money and product gone. I started to cry again but this time not so loud. I had to be good.

Play the Part

I was with the group walking down to the cafeteria for lunch on Saturday. A whole week had passed. It was harder than I thought.

There were new people pacing the floors. This place was bringing them in and sending them out all week long. It was mostly young adults like me but some older people too.

We passed a group of teens. I felt sad for them. This Belmont Center must admit minors too. I knew they were making plenty of money. I was glad that there was only one black kid in that group. Probably because the black crazy minors go to juvie. Other people's kids go to treatment centers. Sad either way.

"Jay is that you?"

Is that who I think it is?

"Mary?" I hugged her. We had been at a few homes together. Been to juvie together. Now we're in an insane asylum together!

Her eyes WERE clearer like Tasha said. She still had a ways to go. She'd put on some weight which looked good on her. This place was helping her.

"My name is Melissa. Don't use my street name here."

I was confused because I had always heard our foster moms call her Mary. Then I remembered in class, our teachers called her Melissa. Damn, no wonder why she messed the fuck up. What happened? I never got the full story.

"What happened to you?" I asked.

"Same thing as you. Nervous breakdown. I called myself trying to get clean. I have gotten into more trouble trying to get clean than when I was in *the life*. It's been one thing after another. But being away from the streets locked up here, my mind is so clear."

She took a breath and smiled.

"I found out who my parents are." My chest heaved as I said that.

We had gotten our lunch and were chatting at a table. Mary's friends joined us. I forgot their names. Mary hugged me before a black nurse said, "No touching please."

Mary knew my story but I never knew hers.

"I met the man who married my folks. They had the wedding on video. I look just like my dad. I couldn't take it. That's when I started tripping."

"THAT would send anyone over the deep end," Mary said. "These pills make me so damn hungry. I gotta chill," she stopped midway through her second plate of beef stroganoff.

"You need to eat. You been a bag of bones for too long," I said. She smiled.

"This is part of you getting clean, having a real appetite."

"No, it's too much. If you're in here another week, you'll start to need a new size of pants."

I laughed. I didn't believe her but she was dead serious. The group wrapped up lunch and they let us go out on the patio.

Ah, the sun, I thought. *What a friend you are.* I watched the crazies play and talk, gossip and walk and wait. That's what you do in a nuthouse. You wait to go the fuck home.

Tim was sitting in my room when I got back from the lunch/recess break. He was visibly still shaken. I hugged him so tight. I fought to keep the tears down.

We talked about nothing. He was doing my assignments while I was in here. Tasha was here but she was visiting Mary at the moment. If I knew Tasha, I knew she was working to get Mary out too. Showing that you have a support system is major in getting out of this place.

Tasha was one of Mary's regular visitors. This would help Mary get out. She had been in here for a month. She was in a different wing at first for those who were suicidal. Once all the drugs left her system and they saw she was no longer violent, they transferred her to my unit. A few more days of good performance and she'd be home free, especially if Tasha was vouching for her.

A well-coiffed, light-skinned black woman wearing a dark gray suit and those pointy toe shoes that look like they hurt, whirled in and gave me a hug.

"Jay, it's so good to see you," she said, excited. She smelled great too.

 She sounded like Tasha. I looked into her eyes. It was Tasha.

"Tasha? Is that you?" I whispered. This Tasha was even prettier than the Tasha I knew.

"Yes, I couldn't come in here in my other work clothes," she laughed. Tim laughed too. Yup, he knew her.

I noticed even Tim was in a suit, looking like his dad. He looked like he had a sermon ready.

Mary came bumbling in. So did Raheem, trying to be nosey.

"You look so good," Tasha said, looking me in my eyes. "The nurses said you've come a long way. I can tell it too."

"Man you look great. My parents send their love," Tim said. That sounded just like what a preacher family would say.

"We offered to clean your apartment but Tasha refused."

"I cleaned it. Everything's ready for you and certain things are locked up," Tasha said with a wink. I hoped Tim didn't catch that.

"Mary, you'll be living with me when you get out," Tasha reported when she turned to her.

"Ya'll just keep showing them you're clear-headed and you'll be out in no time," Tasha said as if we were players on the field getting our next play.

"Take a shower every day. Eat your food. Talk to people. Go to the activities. Stay out of trouble. Your social workers will be talking to you on Monday when they're back in the office."

The white nurse came back to check on us. "Everything okay?"

Raheem was so quiet I forgot he was still in the room.

"Yes. Yes." Tasha straightened up.

"Tim, we've been here long enough. I think we can get going," Tasha said in a voice I didn't recognize. No one can code switch better than a black woman. I don't know who she was pretending to be but even I was convinced this was a different LaTasha Robinson.

Tim embraced me and then Mary after Tasha. Tasha told us she loved us and we said it back. I did love her. Tasha hugged Mary extra long. That hug had more medicine than whatever drugs they was giving Mary. Tim was falling for Tasha.

"See ya'll tomorrow." They headed out into the hallway and walked into the elevator.

Men love the women they ain't got no business being with. If Tasha could get out of *the life*, look how beautiful she could be? Even with all the make-up and multi-colored weaves she wore at the strip clubs and on the Boulevard, she was prettiest today in a regular dress suit. Was she even wearing make-up? She wore one of her *business wigs* that she referenced when she needed to go the DMV or the bank and be taken seriously. It hung down to her shoulders.

As she walked away, other male nurses had to get a look. They talked by the elevator before they headed down. Tasha still had a few more years in *the life* before she was out of it, though. The voice spoke to her too. We had come from the gutter. We didn't deserve to stay there. It had robbed us of so much.

"Who dat bitch?" Raheem abruptly asked, scaring me. I forgot again that he was here. If he wasn't such a pain, I'd say he had the voice of God. It was deep and full.

"Don't call her no bitch. She's an old friend," I said, lying down to think about the last hour of my life.

"She love ya'll. You and Mary. She acts like a Mom. She really cares."

"That's nice of you to say."

"That was your brother? The tall guy?"

"No. Just a friend too."

"Ya'll look alike."

"Not everybody tall and dark skin looks alike," I offered.

"Shut the fuck up," he joked. "Maybe not alike alike but alike."

"Ummmkay."

"That light skin girl looks mighty familiar though. She can get this dick," he joked again, before turning over on his side for his afternoon nap.

His bed faced the window. Mines was closer to the hallway. New screamers had arrived.

"Stop!" I said.

Our worlds—prostitution and drugs—touched so many lives. If you're good at it, you could never really be anonymous. People will recognize you everywhere you go unless you left the state. I decided this was the LAST week I would ever be in a nuthouse.

The Nuthouse

Mary came to my room that night to talk after our evening activity. She stopped tricking as much. Lost her apartment. Lost her car. When she was tricking, she had plenty of money. When she scaled back, her finances were a mess. Her mother was in this place which is why Mary was taken away from their home.

Her mother was a singer and a black activist. Her father broke her mother's heart. He got himself together, got a real job and married a Hispanic woman in San Jose. Her mother was never the same. He told her college was for white people so she didn't go. He told her capitalism was for white people so she didn't work and depended on him.

He never could bring in any money. When he finally woke up, he got a college degree. He entered the legal workforce and married someone who looked nothing like Mary's mother.

Mary eventually got a job at McDonald's. She soon became the manager but wanted to go back to school. She was asking me about Community. Mary graduated from Tearning High School, one of the top high school's in the region. Tasha was a trick. Mary was a woman pretending to be a trick. Mary was too smart to head down the road she was. She was 23 with 5 abortions under her cap. She had no regrets because she hated to think where they'd be if she hadn't had the abortions. They would probably be in foster care from the womb like I was.

I told her about getting into Community and all that they offer. I could've done a commercial for them, the way I was explaining Community to her. Out of the blue, she rubbed my thigh. Raheem was not in the room.

I kept talking about the school because I thought I was either hallucinating or overthinking her touch. I knew this bitch not tryna fuck now. But if she had been in here for a month when she used to taking 10 dicks a day, she had to be burning. I was burning too. Hell, if Tim didn't come in when he did when Tasha was here, I would've taken her right in that bathroom.

Mary's face had filled out and her smile lit up a room. There were not enough candles to shine the way she did. Her peanut butter skin was tempting too.

She rubbed my upper thigh close to my dick. I don't remember ever fucking Mary but it could've happened. She rubbed my dick. Nah, I didn't overthink her touch.

"Mary, leave me alone," I said going to close the door.

She giggled, pulled down her pants and underwear and went into the bathroom. Damn, she must have read my mind.

"We have to make this quick, okay, and you can't be loud like you usually are," she said. So we had fucked before. Damn, drugs sure can fuck up your memory.

Her pussy had tons of hair on it. I had a forest too. I bent her over the sink and went to work. It was Mary who struggled to contain her sound.

She came before me. Hoes are the best because it takes so little to please them. Regular women take hours of training and study. They don't even know what they need to even tell you what they want. Hoes come like dudes.

Mary ran out of the room before I could ask about my performance.

"They're doing roll. I got to go," she said. *Just like in prison*, I thought. I showered her off of me and was already in bed before Raheem and the nurse came in to do the final check for the night.

Raheem lied down after he changed. "I'm going home tomorrow. I know you're glad about that. You can have the whole room to yourself to fuck next time."

My eyes flew open in the darkness. Tomorrow couldn't come fast enough.

"But be careful," he said, in his best version of a whisper. Raheem had such a big voice his whisper was still quite loud.

"If they find you fucking, they'll keep you longer. They get money for every day you stay so they will find reasons to keep you here. That's why Mary been in here so long."

Mary's story was a lie?

"She told me she was in the High Support area because she was going through withdrawals."

"She was going through withdrawals AND fucking people. She wised up and stopped fucking as much."

For some reason, that disappointed me. I thought I was her only one, but it seems Mary had been busy. She went from street drugs to normal drugs and added dick to her cocktail.

Mary! I thought.

"I didn't have sex with her."

"I saw her come into the room. When the door closed, I knew what was going on. Strangely it doesn't smell like sex in here. Boy, that shower must've been lit up!"

"I have no idea what you're talking about. Maybe she was with the dudes next door."

Raheem sighed. He didn't believe me for a second. I was on my side facing the door to our room. I couldn't see his face but I could feel his eyes.

"Alright, liar. Have a good night. Next time get some head. She'll take you to heaven."

I could not wait for that. *Wait a minute. So does that mean she fucked Raheem too? Damn, I didn't mean nothing to her.*

The Truth About my Family

Mary and I had a few more *sessions*. The nurses knew her ways because they were always trailing her when she was around me. She avoided me until she saw the coast was clear.

Tasha and Tim came up here every day. One of the nurses was on to us and told them. Tasha was so mad. She and Tim gathered us together in the very bathroom we fucked in. She turned on the shower to drown out her yelling.

"Y'all nigglets is crazy. You both are one more fuck away from staying another two weeks." This stopped me dead in my tracks. Mary not so much. She could care less.

Tasha called us everything but a child of God. "If y'all don't stop, Tim and I will stop working to get y'all out of here. We both got other things to do."

I heard Raheem come in. His nosey ass.

Tasha lowered her voice. She grabbed the nearby plunger and beat us like kids. Our dumb asses took it even though we both were taller than Tasha who stood at 5'5. She had on those heels again so that gave her a few inches.

I could kill Tasha as I was a whole foot taller than her and Mary had enough meat on her now that she could take her too. Tim walked out of the bathroom and asked Raheem to give us a few minutes.

"This my room, nigga." I realized I hated Raheem because he reminded me of me.

Raheem came in the bathroom to protect me though. Tasha was

still going to work beating us. She was red in the face by this time.

"You cool. Jay?"

She whirled around and was ready to beat Raheem.

"It's cool, Raheem. Just go."

He went alright. He went into the hallway.

"Yo, nurse. These people in here beating Jay and Mary."

Security was called. Nurses whirled around. Tasha's red face gave her away.

Mary and I both lied that she never beat us. Mary's brown arms showed bruises. My dark skin hid my marks. As many times as I've had my ass kicked, Tasha's plunger taps on a Tuesday afternoon was not really a beating. I don't care how many bruises showed.

"She didn't hit us," we said.

"Raheem, why you tell?"

Raheem was supposed to been gone but his Mom *forgot* to pick him up. He's been an ass ever since. He did this to extend our stay. It worked. We both got another two weeks to think about what we did wrong.

Reverend and Mrs. Walker now took Tasha and Tim's spot as they couldn't come. Vanessa, Dan, Dante and Amber came to visit us. Their husbands did most of the talking. The women talked to Mary. Tasha begged the Walkers to visit Mary too or else she would never get out. It was now July.

The older couple filled me in on my family. They weren't too bright. They brought pictures of my Mom and Dad which triggered this whole mess in the first place. Didn't they get that? I could snap but I needed their visibility to get me out. The nurses loved the Reverend and Mrs. Bev brought them cakes and cookies. Reverend was so charming, as most ministers are.

Mary was released three days before me and Tasha and Tim picked her up. Tim was MUCH healthier than her former boyfriends. I really approved of their new relationship. Hopefully, Tim was peeling her off the pole and not profiting from her work. Men date strippers and become pimps because they've never seen so much money. I could see Tim going down that road. I'd have to keep my eye on him. Tasha was no Janet but she was special.

The Reverend was up at Belmont so much they had started a whole new ministry for the nuts. They brought a small group and had a few church services as the afternoon activity. The doctors and nurses loved it. Most people grew up around religion so people were receptive to them. They bought the patients gifts and remembered their names. I can see why my parents wanted them to marry them. The Walkers were such nice people.

They had obtained both of my parents' birth and death certificates. Both of my grandmothers were alive. My mother's mother, Ellen Patterson, lived in El Cerrito, a nice suburb outside of Berkeley. In some spots, you can see the ocean. *Damn*, I thought, *she got out of St. John and didn't think to come get me. Bitch!*

When they found me in my grandmother's house after I had screamed all night long, they couldn't find my birth certificate so the social worker, who must have been a white woman, renamed me. They got me a new social security number and everything.

The Austins, my paternal grandparents, are still alive. The Walkers called them and told them they found me. Reverend Walker was their Pastor when the Walkers lived in Virginia. The Walkers left Virginia when Reverend Walker's insurance business wanted him in the West Coast market. Their house today proved that that was a smart business move.

Even still, the Walkers could have three homes for what they're paying to live in the Pocket of all places. Reverend Walker took a break from pastoring when he moved to California but his newest church in Meadowview is named the same thing as it was in Virginia: Walker Christian Assembly. The church in Virginia had long dissolved within a few years after Reverend and Mrs. Beverly left.

The church took a long time to heal when your parents died. That's why it was easy for me to move on. I left the church with a capable pastor but most of the main people had already moved on. It's no surprise the church folded like it did Reverend Walker told me.

The Austins fought hard to adopt me because they had more resources but my maternal grandmother became unfindable. Changed jobs, changed houses and changed hairdos. I could only imagine trying to grieve the loss of your child and holding onto your living legacy, an infant while uprooting your life to keep the law away. No wonder she went crazy! Because they couldn't find my birth certificate, they couldn't track down the Austins to tell them to come get me.

All four of my grandparents want to meet me. They have been informed of where I am. My mother's father, Christopher Thompson, was a fuck up when my mother was little; wishy-washy at best when she was a young adult but had become *a changed man* says Mr. Walker. I believe it if Mr. Walker says it. He had other children besides my mother Tina.

"Was he the one who walked her down the aisle?"

"No, that was Deacon Smith. He loved your parents. He saw your father grow up and helped to get them their first house. I guess he was a father figure to them, so your mother felt it right to have him participate in the wedding. He and his wife couldn't have children."

"Is he alive?"

"He's old. He was in his 50s when your parents got married."

I remembered the salt and pepper temples. He didn't look at my mother like a dad though. There was a chemistry between those two that you could see even on their wedding day.

It was a Monday and they completely unloaded on me. I knew I was stable because I received the information as just that with no real emotion. Just information to catalog.

I had a lot to think about. I wanted to pace the floor so bad when they left but I knew that would extend my release. I contained myself and pretended I was asleep.

The overnight nurses did their rounds. I laid stiff as a board but I was awake all night. I counted to 100 several times to keep from bursting at the seams. They needed to increase my dosage of Seroquel but they weren't going to find that out from me. I had come too far almost a month in. I could not slip up now.

Two more days to go. *I'm coming home Tasha*, I thought.

Set Free

"I left that nut house and was a changed man. I couldn't be the son of a surgeon and stay in the low life. God changed my life."

"Praise the Lord!" The crowd was on their feet whooping, clapping and praising God. *How long was I on this stage*? I thought. The kids were in the back of the sanctuary waiting for church to end.

I feared the worst. Did I say too much? Did I go too far?

Why were Marcus and Matthew sitting so stiff? Oh Lord. What did I do wrong now? We were in Maryland, a long way from Sacramento. There was no one there from my former life.

"Ok, folks. God has blessed. You are dismissed." Pastor Nickles was ready to go.

People swarmed me. "So what happened next?" Tiffany the praise and worship leader asked.

I gushed and shook my head, moving towards my kids. I didn't feel like unloading any more.

"What happened?"

"Where'd your children come from?"

"How did you end up here though?"

"I think I remember your Mom. She did my probate when I was at Howard."

"She did my probate when I was at Hampton," another AKA

said. My mother was heavily involved in AKA recruitment in college and graduate chapters in the DMV area. I'm not surprised she helped so many women become AKAs, I just didn't know how many of them went to our church.

"Brother Taylor, that was a great testimony. Sometimes we forget where we come from," Pastor Knickles said.

I was the star of the show. The women wanted to know more. I got a few flirtatious grins. The women were intrigued though. Pastor Nickles snatched me out of their one million follow-up questions. You could tell these people were unchurched. You not supposed to ask all these probing questions after a testimony like that. I had told them more than enough.

"What drugs were you on?"

"You didn't go to prison though."

"I used to go to Walker Christian Assembly. Are they still living?"

"Were you a Blood or Crip?"

"How did you get into Optometry?"

"Why didn't you become a surgeon like your daddy? That would've made him proud."

"Y'all leave him alone. I got plans for him. Y'all gonna run him off. Y'all head home," the Reverend barked.

"Pastor, he gotta finish on Sunday." Only a praise and worship leader as good as Tiffany could say that to Pastor.

"I know. I'm trying to invite him back if you shut up," he laughed.

They turned and left me alone. I was not coming back to tell the rest. They would just have to learn to get to know me. With my sons in tow, I followed Pastor Nickles as he walked out the building. His new wife was already in the car.

"Pastor, I can't tell more. This was a lot tonight."

"We've never had so many people tuned in to our live stream as tonight. There were 800 people watching this on a Friday night. 800 people! We're lucky if we get 15 people. Please think about it."

"Nah, I'm good."

"Your story may go viral by tomorrow morning."

Matthew and Marcus had carried Jonathan to the car. Marcus was already gone. Probably to see Sis. Dana, the Kids Kamp Director. She was quite pretty tonight for a Friday night service. I figured she was a little older than him but we'll see.

Pastor didn't know social media. I would've needed a few more views than that to go viral. Pastor was eager to blow up. That's what I couldn't stand about young pastors. They hungry for all the wrong things.

"Ok, Imma pray for you that you change your mind." Pastor Nickles prayed too well. I knew I was doomed.

When I got in the car, I had one message in messenger. It was Tasha.

I was back in the office on Monday. Everyone looked happy to see me. I'm sure the rumor was prime, pumped and well worked over this weekend especially with Chris. He can't hold no water.

 "Buddy, you okay?" He asked by my office.

"Yup, I had a busy weekend." I was about to have a busy morning. I had four patients in a row before lunch. I welcomed the distraction.

I waited for him to get the hint but he was still in my office. He closed the door.

"I went out with Melissa," he said as he pulled up a chair.

"Who?"

"Your friend from Olive Garden."

I remembered. I wanted to know what the fuck Chris was gonna do with all that ass Mary had.

"When?"

"We met for a quick brunch. She paid a babysitter to have coffee and breakfast with me." He seemed so proud of himself.

"Her skin is so creamy."

My how the wheels have turned. White men actually think it's okay to brag about their black female conquests in front of a black man. I wanted to punch him in the teeth. I wondered if this is how he felt when I bragged about the white women I went out with. Like he wished I'd kept this one to myself.

"I reimbursed her for the babysitter. She was so easy to talk to."

Mary had won Chris over. She was always charming. Their kids were around the same age and they were both divorced so I'm sure conversation came easy.

"Chris, my first patient is walking down the hall. I gotta go," I said headed to the door of my office. Chris got the point.

"Now you know how it feels," he said quietly but loud enough for me to hear. I ignored him and went into the exam room. *That nigga*, I thought.

The Time Had Come

I was grateful for that full busy Monday. Pastor Nickles texted me on Saturday. He decided to preach instead of asking me to come up a second time.

Thank you, God, I thought.

"Thank you for letting me know," I answered back. I nearly danced out of my skin.

He definitely received something from the Lord because service was on fiyah. He used my testimony a little too much but the message was awesome. I don't care for the music so much. Just preach my head off is all I require. Pastor Nickles stay offending us. I loved it.

Tasha and I were having slow text-only conversations. I was scared because I loved her. She now lived in Philadelphia with her Mom. When she told me that, I thought she was still tricking. Nothing could be further from the truth. She too found God.

Tasha was divorced with kids, like seemingly everybody in their 40s. Love is rough, shit. She had teenagers. Her son was giving her a little trouble so she asked me how to handle him. I gave some Mr. Belvedere advice.

I looked through her pictures. She had a *glow up* as the kids say. She was now a well sought after music teacher and a Zumba and pole dancing instructor at a local gym. Her plate seemed to be running over.

With Jonathan, I was knee-deep in little leagues. I'd moved Mrs. Bev into my home after the Reverend died five years ago. She was 81 but was quite nimble. She was my other baby.

Tim never shaped up. Vanessa and her family moved to Richmond, VA, the place where it all began to be closer to her mother. Vanessa and Dan ended up having five kids. Amber and Dante also moved several times before settling in Charlotte, NC. They had three children. The baby she was carrying when I met her is now 20 years old studying at NYU.

Five Years Ago

After I had come out of the nuthouse, the Walkers took me in. They asked me a thousand times was I okay. My classes helped to keep me out of trouble. I was still selling then because I was not going to take on any debt for these dumb ass classes. Maybe down the road for my real classes for my major, but not for *Intro to Studying*.

My mother's parents came to meet me within a month of me staying at the Walkers and it was like they never left. I had Tim's parents and my maternal grandparents straight out spoiling me. I received it all. I had 20 years to make up for. My grandmother and Mrs. Walker became such good friends. This was only the beginning.

I took out the garbage. I fired their white groundskeeper and mowed the lawn. They hired him back after a few weeks. He was not a gardener but was an artist.

Every time Mrs. Bev added items to the grocery list on the fridge, I gave her money to buy groceries or bought them myself. She never asked where I got the money. Vanessa knew.

"Don't bring that shit around here," she said, looking me dead in my eye.

Shit? She don't talk like that, I thought.

I had plenty of customers already within the first four months. Most used to trek to South Sac for their stashes. Now, for some, I'm around the corner. They done told their friends I was nearby. I don't know what it is. Customers found me no matter what I did. I wondered if there was a *Come to me I have drugs* sign across my forehead because I was getting new people daily even though I was cleaner now than ever in my whole life.

I wanted to stop slanging but the money was getting too good. In Pocket, I could charge so much more for my shit.

I stayed out of the house most of the day. That kept the goons from finding me. I didn't want no danger to hit the Walkers' house on account of me. I doubled up on classes and was knocking out my general education courses. Nobody wanted to see an able-bodied man in his 20s laying around the house all day. Getting out of the house helped me go back to my own house and check on business too. Working and school helped me heal.

"The doctor says it takes a full year to recover from a nervous breakdown," Reverend Walker reported.

I felt an inner incision heal one stitch at a time, day by day. I was only taking Seroquel. I was on 400mg per night which the doctor said was still very high. My anxiety must be through the roof even being babied by with the Walkers. I ate a lot.

"If we have to stay at 400mg for you to be stable, then that's what we'll do." He said it so cute but he was not walking around with an extra 30 lbs. The women loved it. Apparently, I was no longer crackhead skinny. I was no longer shopping in the kids' section for clothes.

That night was coming back to me in pieces. I did try to run up to the second floor. Dante became Jackie Joyner Kersey. He flew over me up 'dem steps and had them kids locked in the farthest room from the stairs.

The kids were screaming. The men, including the cops, had restrained me and taken me into the ambulance. I was trying to catch my grip because I did not want the cops near me. I couldn't get another strike. I would be off to prison.

Damn near all of Pocket was in this little cul-de-sac trying to figure out what was going on.

God knows what they were thinking. These niggas. Can't have nothing.

A neighbor tried to come over and see what was going on. Mrs. Bev knew the deal.

"Excuse me, we're fine. My son just needs a little help right now. Thank you," she said, directing her away. I loved that woman.

I later found out that her and the Reverend went around to all the neighbors and gave them some banana pudding and wine. Rich people's way of apologizing to their neighbors, I guess.

A lot of the decorations that I saw when I first came in the house were gone. I left their home in tatters. Vanessa did not mince words about what the Walkers were sacrificing having me here after I tore up their house. I had to keep my business off their property.

Tim grew jealous of all the time his parents were spending with me. He thought I was taking his place. He was so damn dumb. I lived with them for two years. Tim hated it every day.

He didn't know how to be a son. I went with them to the movies, fixed their cars and fixed the appliances Reverend didn't feel like tending to. I bought them new electronics when what they had gave out. I was going to earn my keep. I owed them my life. I even started going to their church. They were so easy to love.

I studied every picture, every video, everything about my parents. All the cards and resolutions sent to Reverend Walker when my parents died. Both of my parents were well-loved. In the 30+ years they lived, they added so much value to the world and here their little nigglet was poisoning now two fucking communities. *A surgeon's son shouldn't be doing this.* That voice haunted me.

I spent Thanksgiving at the Walkers. Tasha and Mary were able to come. Tasha and Tim were never an item or they broke up. They avoided each other like the plague. My paternal grandparents, Patricia and Ed Austin flew in from Richmond. It was a reunion in so many ways. The Austins hadn't seen the Walkers in two decades. I had gained quite a bit of weight so I really looked like my dad.

Mom Pat, what she told me to call her, would not let me go. Her and Mrs. Bev had the same response. They had seen a ghost.

"You don't have to call me Grandpa. I'm okay with Mr. Ed for now," he said, trying to shake my hand.

"I've waited all my life for a family. You gon be Pop Pop starting now," I said. I pushed his hand away and gave him a hug. He was beaming.

Everyone gave us some time to ourselves in the living room while they stayed in the kitchen and the dining room. Amber had a baby girl named Hope. Tasha and Mary loved Baby Hope. Amber was a little nervous about sharing her baby with Tasha and Mary given their occupations, but she eventually let go.

"I'll give her a good scrubbing later, so I guess it's alright," she said slyly.

"Amber!" Vanessa chided.

Mary and Tasha no longer wanted to hold the baby. That was the only damper on the whole night.

"Brian!" Pat wailed. She grabbed me and rocked me like I was a baby. My head was on her large bosom. The death of my father mixed with age had not been kind to either of them. They were a little younger than the Walkers but they looked older than the Walkers by far.

"For this day we waited. Thank you Lord!" she cried out loud. We all were a big ball of goo.

Granddad Ed just held my hand. He was a proud man but the tears streamed down his face. This was closure for them. It was the beginning for me.

I asked if my maternal parents could come so everybody would be together. The Reverend said, in so many words, that my grandmothers didn't get along well, given that my mom's mom Ellen caused all of this.

"It would be best for there to be one reunion at a time." I never even thought to blame Mom Ellen. I just thought it was just a bad chain of events. But once I thought about it, her being so possessive of me and going into hiding to prevent me from going back to Virginia, yeah, she did fuck it up. She fucked it up for everybody, especially me. Fucking bitch.

After the Austins and I had gathered ourselves together, we sat at the table for dinner and ate. They followed me around like puppies. When they got tired of me, Mrs. Bev and Mom Pat got caught up and Pop Pop and Reverend Walker got caught up. The Austins were in town until Tuesday, the next day. They were staying at the house.

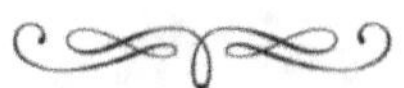

House for Sale

Their beautiful home in Pocket was sold for millions which helped to pay for Mrs. Bev's care. Those proceeds and that hefty life insurance policy made Mrs. Bev was a rich woman. Because Vanessa and Amber had huge families and I just had only Jonathan at that point, my house was the obvious choice for Mrs. Bev to move to.

Tim was still in California being a pain in everybody's ass. He just had to be rebellious. He knew everybody's on the East Coast, living well on half and a third of what he's paying for that bummy one-bedroom apartment in Natomas, but he kept bragging about it. We had all offered for him to live with us until he got a security gig.

'He insisted on staying in California. He was still a bachelor at the ripe old age of 49. Janet, his old thing, was married to a man from Montana. They lived on a huge ranch there with their three biracial kids. Everybody was mixing nowadays. Janet still called Mrs. Bev from time to time. They remained friends despite Tim.

Jonathan was the true healing agent for Mrs. Bev. They were thick as thieves. She let him get away with everything. She was the mother he needed since his mother could be so flaky.

We had a few drop-in patients in the afternoon. I was managing my memories and them while checking my messages for Tasha's voice. I was taking it easy but I wanted to see her again. I really hoped she was the one but I knew all too well not to get too excited.

At a minimum, I'd love to see her again. Between finding my kids, getting married and divorced and building my career, my 20s and

30s were just as traumatizing as the first 21 years I spent before knowing who I was. At 41, I just wanted someone to be my resting place.

How cool it would be if Tasha and Mary/Melissa linked up?

Oh God. What are you up to? I thought.

I was packing up to go. Jamir came into my office to chat which was surprising because he was a card-carrying introvert. I looked at the time. It was 5:49 pm. Jamir had a whole eleven minutes to get out my damn face.

"I saw you at your church on Friday."

I didn't realize I held my breath until I started talking again.

"Oh yeah? I was as surprised as you. My Pastor put me on the spot but it is what it is."

Apparently, he had follow-up questions too. "So how'd you end up graduating from New England?"

"I stayed with a cousin while I was in Boston. Once I was out of California, I was good."

He was a bit disappointed.

"So you don't do nothing? Not even sell?" He was looking for a plug.

"Nigga get out my face," I said, heading towards the door. He stopped me before I crossed the threshold.

"We didn't have this conversation."

"Your secret's safe if my secrets are safe," I said.

He paused before allowing me to pass. "We cool."

I never liked him.

I got quite a few texts from women in the church. Some encouraging. Others were damn right pornographic. Women love bad boys.

I screenshotted all the bad ones and sent them straight to First Lady Nickles. The offenders called me everything but a child of God for telling on them. I sent screenshots of those messages to Lady Nickles too. All messages stopped by Wednesday. I guess word had gotten out that I was not playing that shit.

Thursday night Bible Study was uncomfortable as some of the perpetrators were in the audience with me. Women who were usually friendly avoided me like the plague. Old nasty selves.

First Lady Nickles thanked me for the screenshots. Some of those women sent stuff to Pastor. A few of them were not even members so she couldn't even kick them out of our church. The ones who were had been sat down. Pastor Nickles was good for an old fashioned disciplinary sit-down. He'd have people sit down for six months. He hoped they'd get so mad that they'd leave on their own which most did. Some waited it out and ministered better after the sit down than before which means it was effective.

Mary/Melissa texted me. "Lunch Saturday? My kids are 8, 10 and 5. Chuckie Cheese?"

Jonathan could play with the five-year-old.

"Sure," I said. "Do you like Chris?" I asked.

"I'on know yet. He did a pretty good job blowing my back out, so there's that."

Mary/Melissa even all dolled up and educated hadn't changed one damn bit.

You could always tell when he had just had sex when he came to work. He didn't walk in, he floated. I didn't feel like hearing about Mary tomorrow. I braced myself because I knew it was coming.

"TMI Mary," I texted back. "I'm near the Chuckie Cheese on Adeline Road."

"Let's do it. You from California so I know how flaky y'all asses can be."

"Lol," I replied.

That's one of the benefits of moving back to the East. People are firm and direct. I knew I was home when people weren't so easily offended by how I spoke or that I expected people to keep their word. I'm sure Mary had to relearn this East Coast toughness. I had too. It came natural to me because it was in my blood but I still had to work on it for a few years. That *flakiness* could cost you all kinds of opportunities. All my young life people told me I talked too loud or I was too direct. When I found out my father was from the DMV area, it all made sense.

"Oh yeah, I saw your little live stream, Mr. Preacher."

Oh no! I thought. *Who the hell had seen this live?* I couldn't even ask Chris if he'd seen it because his nosey ass would go looking for it if he hadn't.

"You could've left my name out. It's okay. Mary could be anybody in California," she replied.

"I apologize. I was in the moment." I genuinely was sorry. I can't imagine what she thought of what I said about her.

I still couldn't bring myself to watch it. Matthew and Marcus didn't know about all the foster home stuff. They didn't know I was that deep in the life. They met me when I was sobered up and fat. They said I did a good job but the things I shared explained a lot.

"When are you going to tell the rest of your story, though?" She asked. I couldn't answer that. Damn.

Pastor Nickles concluded Bible Study. He sat down beside me after the benediction. I was still texting Mary, my elbows on my knees with no clue if or when I would finish my story.

The sanctuary had emptied out. He had received hate mail. People said I was *dusty*, he was *dusty* and Tim was *dusty*. They said Tasha was a fool to help me and was a *Mammy* for doing so. Tasha and Mary were *thots*.

A few Asian Facebook groups got wind of the Live and said I said racist things regarding the hospital staff. Some people said that Pastor and I *looked gay* which is code for we *looked civilized*. With Black people, you're either a thug or gay. Older pastors messaged him, even formally wrote him, scolding him to never do that again unless he knew the testimony about to come forth. The live a week later stood at 20,000 views. For an hour-long video, that was huge for Pastor Nickles. *What the hell did I say?*

Nonetheless, most of the responses had been, "What happened next?"

I still was trying to figure out why I was *dusty* and how *pancakes* had anything to do with Tasha. Pastor was trying to do another Facebook Live. How could anyone give a politically correct testimony?

"No one's contacted you other than our members?" Pastor asked, referring to the nudes I got.

"Not that I know of," I said and started scrolling thru my phone. I noticed some hidden messages in my Messenger. I hated that part of Messenger. It was usually spam but I saw that it had some inflammatory messages.

Damaged Beyond Repair

Black men ain't shit, periodt.

My Pastor would've shot you trying to go up 'dem steps.

Are Tasha and Mary still alive?

Was her real name Mary or Melissa?

Fake news. Stop looking for a book deal.

You sucked my dick in juvie?

I remember you.

Hey, Jay. It's Ms. Lacreasha.

Two local news outlets contacted me. The Howard campus newspaper contacted me. The alumna over the newspaper pledged AKA with my Mom. She was 64 and still working. This was all sitting in my phone. I turned it down quickly as if it was on fire. Pastor Nickles was sitting right next to me reading all the good, bad and ugly that came through. I had at least 1,000 new friend requests. They were going to be sorely disappointed as I barely post anything. But I remembered my sons. Marcus was in grad school; Matthew and Luke were in college. Jonathan was only six but even he knew his way around some of these social media sites even though I didn't teach him that. He's never on it at home with me, yet I know he knows what's going on. The kids at school must tell him. They could eat him alive. Kids could be cruel if they found out your parent was a thug or a ho. I know, I was that bully.

Yet, none of my kids came to me about any type of backlash. maybe the story wasn't as big a deal as I was making it out to be. Hopefully, it wasn't. That would be terrible for all of my kids.

"This is a book deal," Pastor Nickles said. He came from the streets too. That ability to smell money never dies. "Keep playing."

"Look here." He showed me screenshots of women's *secret* groups discussing all sides of the video. How I was selling drugs and hosting orgy parties when there were three churches in the vicinity. How God used Tim, the family reject, to reunite the families, his and mine. How the Walkers turned a bad situation and birthed a new ministry into their church—Blessings at Belmont.

Jamir regularly schooled us on social media. Twenty thousand views were not a lot of views for such a long video. People from all over the country had seen the video. #BrianAustin was trending. Foster care groups had gotten a hold of it. Pastor was a praying man but he was also a businessman. "We have to strike while the iron's hot."

"Pastor, LaTasha and Melissa have already contacted me. They're nervous." No they wasn't. I was.

"They're both professional women. I don't want to cause them no trouble."

"Mary and LaTasha are some of the most common names ever. No one's going to find them unless they speak up." He knew I was lying.

"My oldest kids are starting their careers. I don't want them to lose out on opportunities because this got messy…er."

Pastor Nickles knew I had a point.

"On Sunday, we will finish the story." He told me in the most direct way I ever heard him speak to me. His thug collar was hanging lose tonight. He got up after looking me dead in my face for what seemed like hours, but was only minutes, and left the sanctuary.

"I'm not coming," I said, loud enough so he could hear.

He ignored me. "Come along. I'm cutting the lights out."

I got up to leave. I heard First Lady Nickles ask in a whisper, "What he say?"

"It don't even matter."

They had the new ring security system at the church. They let me leave by myself. When I got into the atrium to leave, Pastor Nickles said from the alarm speaker, "When you get outside, use your keys and pretend like you locking the doors. Then go to your car."

"Ok," I said as I followed his instructions. He probably was watching me from his house not too far from here. *That was weird,* I thought. Him being able to see me like that.

When I got in the car, I checked my voicemail. My grandmother, my Mom's mom, Mom Ellen, called and said she left a message. Baby Boomers. They hate to text. How did I miss her call?

I loved Mom Ellen. On her message, she talked for a minute catching me up on Tim. He had taken her on as a mother. That's the only reason I bother with him. Mom Ellen is the only person who seems to be able to deal with his blockhead ass. They watch out for each other.

Mom Ellen told me she had a boyfriend and Tim had a new girlfriend. She paused and then her tone changed. She said through a softened voice:

> *Jay, a person called me from a scam like number. Tim traced it to a 202 area code. The woman said bum bitch mother and hung up. It was a woman but what is a bum bitch mother? I asked Tim if he knew what that was about. He said I should talk to you like he knows something is going on. Do you? I want you to listen to it to see if you recognize the voice. Call me.*

That would be the last time I'd hear Pastor Nickles voice, at least for a little bit. This story had to die.

I was actually considering sharing more of my story but when Mom Ellen told me she was being contacted by internet trolls, that was too much. I called Pastor Nickles' about the situation and he reluctantly agreed to let it go. This wasn't just me I was exposing.

Burying the Truth

"Got plans with Mary tonight," Chris beamed. *This nigga*, I thought as I stirred my coffee. It was Tuesday and a few people texted me from the church. Deacon Brown scolded me even though he knew I was putting my grandmother and others first in an attempt to keep them out of harm's way.

"God would've protected them," he said. I didn't care. I had an obligation to protect them too.

Pastor Nickles and Deacon Brown didn't believe the grandma story. They thought I was lying and being a punk. Clearly, Pastor had put him up to it because Pastor knew he could never talk to me like Deacon Brown could. I didn't care if Pastor was disappointed but hearing Deacon Brown upset unnerved me. But I hated that Deacon Brown was willing to do Pastor's dirty work. Church folk can be such bitches.

"Things are getting serious," I said to Chris, pretending to care.

"She's my girlfriend," he said matter-of-factly. "I love her skin."

"I bet you do. You know she used to do drugs," I said and regretted it as soon as it slipped out. That was none of my business to tell him. I just hated that this marginally attractive temperamental white divorcé got Mary; the new and improved Mary too. Not the Mary I knew 20 years ago. There was definitely a brain drain happening with black people. The brightest and best of black women were running into the arms of whitey.

"Yeah, she told me. Our kids really mesh which is sometimes hard in blended families," Chris informed me like he was talking to a 10-year-old.

"She put everything on the table because she feared you would spill the beans. You know, she wasn't the only one doing drugs," Chris said knowingly as he stirred his coffee without looking me in my eye.

Bitch, I thought.

"I sold a little in college but I was young. You know everyone has a past. So who am I to judge?" He said. "Jesus forgives, right?" He said, tapping me on the shoulder.

"So she didn't tell you about me?" I asked, again regretting that as soon as the words came out of my mouth. Chris couldn't keep a secret if you paid him too.

"No," Chris said flustered. "What? You did drugs too?" He asked, looking me up and down.

Clearly, I didn't look like the type. That is the greatest compliment an ex-drug dealer could receive.

I shook my head no. Now I was flustered. I didn't understand how Mary could talk about her past without including mine.

"What exactly did Mary tell you?"

"She refused to tell me about you. She kept saying *that's his business to tell*. She just told me about her own shit."

Now I really feel bad for telling Mary's business. She could've given so much ammunition to destroy my career and she didn't. I'm such a jackass.

"You still want her after what she told you?" I asked. Why am I still being rude?

"She's gorgeous and fun so yes. She told me about the drugs but that was it," he said. He lowered his voice and waited until Anna, our other partner, came and left the breakroom before continuing in a lowered voice. "Is there more?"

"No," I said, shaking my head profusely. Mary had left out the tricking, stripping and the 3-month stint in the looney bin. I wasn't gonna tell him more since she didn't tell my business. Why did I open up this can of worms?

"Josh, if you know something tell me. We're supposed to be friends," he said a little louder than I was comfortable with. "What is it?"

I was friends with Chris but Mary was family. I had already said too much. He was just going to have to be mad at me.

"That's her business to tell."

"So there is more?"

I headed out of the breakroom. I had a few kid patients to get in character for.

"Jay? Josh?" He cried out as he trailed me.

"It's nothing."

"You're full of shit." Chris smelled blood. "Did you two ever sleep together?"

"Absolutely not," I lied.

"Why should I expect the truth out of you? Your name isn't even Josh," he said.

I stopped in my tracks. What did he know? Mary didn't know who my real family was. Did he see me on the church live? We're not friends on social media. I am vigilant about keeping my co-workers away from that stuff but you just never know what people have seen.

"What's that supposed to mean?" I said incredulously containing my rage.

He pursed his lips. "You know exactly what it means, you fucking liar," he said quietly. trailing me as I headed to my office.

"Chill out guys," another partner said as we got closer to the nurses and patient.

I walked straight into my first appointment. I heard Chris stop and as I turned into the exam room. I could see Chris still looking at me. I could feel his eyes burning holes through my back.

Shit, I thought.

A Lunch Playdate

Wednesday was a full day. It had been two weeks since Chris and I had our altercation in the breakroom. We stopped talking to each other. Mary had texted me that night.

"Keep my name out of your mouth. I really like Chris. Don't mess this up for me." She wrote.

"Yes, Ma'am."

"When are we going to go to lunch? Maybe we can do a play date. Your youngest is close to my kids' age."

"I'll let you know," I replied.

"Well, forget you then," she fussed. I didn't think it was appropriate for us to go on a lunch date without Chris.

"I just don't want Chris to be offended. He really likes you. There's some things I need to share with you that he doesn't need to know about."

"Like what?"'

"It's not something you text."

"MARY! Stop playing." The truth is I didn't trust myself with Mary. She had aged backwards and I didn't want to run the risk of sliding in between their relationship. I was jealous of Chris. Mary had truly transformed. She was my type of woman too.

"Do you remember a girl named Tiara? We used to dance together. She went by the name of Destiny. Brown-skinned but darker than me. Kinda tall but peach-shaped?"

"No." Mary just described damn near 90% of the women I fucked when I was in *the life*.

"She had curly hair," Mary said. "Like she had a little bit of something else in her family."

"No."

"She rolled with Rani and Nikki. She went to Milton, I believe."

"I'm drawing another blank." I seriously don't remember several periods in my life.

These names meant nothing to me. When my older sons ask me about my childhood and teen years, there are some periods I draw complete blanks on. The heavy drugs and depression had wiped my memory clean in some spots. Plus, when you in that life, you don't care enough about people to remember names and friends. It's safer to not get attached. They were all faceless creatures.

She didn't text back after that.

I came home swamped. I usually try and avoid the after-work nap because it messes with my sleep, but between my patients and my kids, I was tapped out. I called myself taking a cat nap.

A memory came to me while I was asleep. I saw myself on a bench in a park. I had to be 20 years old. I felt death near.

I had lived a hard life. My lips were black. I used my stash to go to sleep. I felt like I was going to die very soon. I had all my money on me. I was looking for someone to give it to because I knew I was going to die soon.

In this large park, Clark Park, with empty benches all over, a short fat black woman sat next to me. We sat there for a good 20 minutes before she started talking about the weather. It was the fall but it's California so the weather is not as hot a topic as in areas where they have actual seasons.

"Ma'am, I'm going to die real soon," I said after we stopped shooting the breeze.

"How you know that?" Her heavy voice asked. Even as an older woman, she was very pretty.

"I just know. You need money?"

"Why?" She turned to me inquisitively.

"This is all the money I have," I said, taking out my wad of cash from my pocket, giving it to her.

She looked at it. She looked back at me.

"But you gon need it, though."

"Ma'am, death is real close. I want a good person to have my money. I know you could use it. Everybody needs money."

"What's your name?"

"Joshua but everyone calls me Jay."

"How you gon have a name like Joshua and be a nobody?"

"Ma'am, take the money."

"Son, listen to me. There is gonna be a death but you will live to be an old man," she said.

"You won't be like me and your father if you act right," she insisted while hitting me on the arm.

"Ma'am, please."

"Son, I see it. Save that money. You're gonna need it later."

"Ma'am, here's your last chance. Death is close."

"Believe me, you're gonna need that money. Keep it."

I got up to leave.

"My name is Tina. Remember my name," she said as I walked away.

She started to yell.

"Remember my name!"

She said it as loud as I could hear it until I was out of the park.

"Dad! Dad!" Matthew and Jonathan woke me up.

"What?"

"You're crying."

I felt the tears running down my face.

"My mother visited me when I was about to die."

After a few slices of pizza and Matthew and Marc's failed attempts to understand what I was saying, they gave up. I had turned into mush every time I thought of that woman. Matthew took me up to my bedroom and tucked me in like a baby. I called out for the rest of the week. I knew if I started pacing again I would be back in someone's nuthouse. I had to contain myself but I just couldn't.

"Thank you, Mama."

Hot Times in the City

Today was the day. Those days off were just what the doctor ordered. By Sunday, I was good to go. After months of texting and Face Timing, Tasha and I were going out on a real date. We took it slow but there was definitely still chemistry. I just hoped it wasn't too weird. I tried not to show my excitement but my sons were onto me.

 Marc had gotten me some new cologne.

"The ladies love this stuff," Marc assured me. I chuckled.

Matthew shined up my shoes. Luke was in town. He lived with his mother, Nicole. He was conceived in the San Francisco Bay but they moved around a lot since Nicole was in the Navy. She retired and made a living in Norfolk, Virginia as she crossed over from military to civilian life. Luke went to Hampton University. He was smart enough to go to Harvard but Hampton gave him a free ride.

I always loved having all my boys under one roof. Luke was so wise for his age. Not street smart like Marc. Luke had some unique gifts that my other sons did not have. He was the only one of my sons who was raised with his mother and man was there a difference in his temperament. He didn't have nearly as much bitterness in his heart as Marc and Matthew. He had some bitterness which thawed as we grew closer. He was his mother's son as he should be. He, like Matthew, was jealous of Marc 's relationship with me.

"It took a long time for Dad to become Dad," Marc exclaimed one night when they were in another round of *who had it worse.*

"It was rough at first. I had to learn how to be a son and he had to learn how to be a dad. That was no fun."

They didn't get it because when they really started coming around, I had finally grew up. I cooked, cleaned, shuttled Marc to practices and pediatrician visits. Marc and I grew up together.

Marc and Matthew had to continually remind Luke what he did have. His own mother—a damn good mother and a great stepdad. He had been all over the world. He had several scholarships to choose from when he was looking for colleges. When Luke and his mother were in the same room, you could tell they adored one another. I came into his life in his teens when he really needed his mom to cut the cord. Nicole was having hard time letting her husband Rasheed help Luke transition into manhood and Luke wasn't the type of son to tell his mother to back up, which is probably why he was her favorite. Rasheed thanked me.

"I got my wife back," he said.

Luke and Nicole were becoming an item in an uncomfortable way. Nicole had girls with her husband but she didn't love them like she did *Lukey*. Rasheed's girls, even as pre-teens, made boundaries with their mother. Nicole married a man who was very much like her son—a pushover.

Jon may have some bitterness in the future too but he spends two to four days a week with his mother Joanna, my ex-wife. I try to be as liberal as possible with Joanna's time. What I would give to spend five minutes with the woman who gave me life! I'm sure it's still not the same as having your mother around 24/7. People bash single mothers but what any foster or adopted kid wouldn't give to have one single biological parent raising them and keeping them out of the system. When you're an orphan, you envy the children of single mothers. That was privilege. You cannot put a price on spending time with your own mother.

Also, when Jon is away, I can give my older sons more attention. Lord knows they needed as much, or more, molding as Jon did. I broke them and had to put them back together. There were conversations we could have as men without having to keep up with Jon. Joanna had a younger son, James Jr., by her husband. James Jr. was three-years old. Jon needed as much time with other kids as he could get. If the boys had their way, they would be together all the time.

"We're going to keep it PG," I assured my older boys.

"Bullshit," Marc quipped.

"Watch your mouth," I said. "How do I look?"

They researched Tasha. They all thought she was a beauty even in her 40s.

I had on a suit and tie. A man cannot go wrong with a suit and tie. It was a powder blue shirt with a dark blue paisley tie which complimented my skin whenever I wore it under a black suit.

I got a fresh haircut. My maternal grandfather, Chris, still has a head full of hair. My peers didn't need haircuts as often now that they were older. I seemed to need them more. I had my barber add color. Greys never start in the back. They always have to come front and center to remind you that the clock is ticking.

"Great, Dad," Matthew assured me. "Now, hurry up."

I had to drive two hours to get to the restaurant that Tasha let me choose. I remembered Tasha loved seafood, so we went to the Charthouse on the Philadelphia waterfront. Philadelphia was having the last of its Summer Solstice outdoor concert series at Penn's Landing. Dinner and an outdoor concert sounded good.

"Ok, I'm gone. Put Jon to bed by 8:30 at the latest."

Even if I wasn't gonna get laid, I was gonna use that hotel room and drive straight to work from Philadelphia. I grabbed my overnight bag and was out the door. I was so happy.

While driving into Philadelphia Mary texted me.

"Have fun on your date," she wrote.

"I will."

"She's so excited. So come correct or I will have to put hands on you."

"My sons got me together. I know what to do," I assured her.

"Tasha is not who she was so don't expect that on a first date," Mary schooled me.

Shit, I thought. It had been a whole four months since I got some pussy and what I got wasn't even that good. Hopefully, Tasha would reconsider.

"I know," I said after a few moments of distress.

I was 20 minutes away when Tasha texted me, *Omw.*

Just getting off the expressway. I'll be there soon too, I texted back.

The Philadelphia PD was out in full force tonight. Clearly, they had some bills to pay. I had to keep my phone down. It was 4:30

pm and it was rather quiet on Delaware Ave. I loved the Philadelphia skyline. Philadelphia and New York had to have the best skylines in the world. I took deep breaths as I rolled into the parking lot.

I'm here, Tasha texted.

Just pulled in too.

It's show time, I said to myself. I was excited and terrified. No matter what happened, I was determined to have a good time tonight.

I got out the car that was waxed due to Luke's insistence and headed to the door. I saw her waiting for me. At that moment, I knew she was the one I was waiting for.

We talked about our kids, divorces, professions (she worked as a social worker which I could tell she loved) and caught up on old friends' whereabouts. We talked about everything. We didn't make it to the concert. We chatted like old friends but ran to the hotel room like old lovers. I took some Viagra® right after dinner as she kept running her foot up my leg. I had to restrain myself as the waiter brought the check. It had been a couple of months of *celibacy* for Tasha and, true to form, she was in need of some *Vitamin D*. I did not want to disappoint.

The hotel room was right on the water and overlooked the Delaware River. The view must have been an aphrodisiac because Tasha was naked within the blink of an eye.

"I've lost 30 pounds in these last few months waiting for you to ask me out on a date. I didn't want you to turn me down for any reason," she confessed.

Even at 40, Tasha was still quite firm and... tight. I was surprised I hung in there that long. I knew either I was moving to Philadelphia or she was moving to Maryland. I didn't tell her I took up running again to train for her.

"Girl, come here," I said and we were off to the races again.

An Unexpected Turn

I was a minute late getting into work.

"Damn, it was that good, huh?" Chris said in jest. He broke his silent treatment of the past few weeks.

"I see Mary told you about my date," I said, irritably.

"She sure did. You needed it. You've been uptight for a few weeks."

"Get out my face, nigga," I said, glad to have my friend back.

I was floating. Tasha wore my old ass out just like the doctor ordered. Even my boys noticed a difference when I came home.

"Damn Dad. You didn't even call to check up on us. That's how we knew you had fun,'" Luke said.

Luke's mother had made advances toward me but I felt it would not be fair to marry one of the older boys' mothers. She had gotten clean and was still quite a looker. Luke always seemed to be overly interested in my conquests, telling me how his mom would be a better fit. Even when I was marrying Jonathan's mom, he was advertising his mother and I getting back together.

"Was she fat? Did she talk too much?" Luke asked, looking for an angle.

"Stop. Get over it," I said, looking him square in his face. "It will never happen."

He hated that it would never happen. Hated it to the core. I looked at my phone and noticed I had six messages from my former mother-in-law.

Please call me, she finally texted me.

"Jonathan, have you heard anything from your mother today?" I yelled up the steps.

"No," he yelled from his room. He already had homework and projects he was working on.

I called Grace, Jonathan's maternal grandmother. "What's going on?"

"Sit down," she directed.

"Mom!" I loved my mother-in-law. Her daughter was a pill. A bi-polar pill.

"Joshua, please. This is important and I need you to hear me. Joshua, she's gone."

"Who?" I asked, hoping it wasn't Joanna, my ex-wife.

"Joanna. Joshua, Joanna's dead."

"Joanna!"

"She killed herself. She was pregnant," Mom Grace said softly and with sadness.

"She left a suicide note. You should come and get it," she continued. By this time, the phone was out of my hand and I could barely hear her. Jon had run into the kitchen for some cookies.

"Dad? Dad, what's wrong?" Matthew asked. He grabbed the

phone.

"Hello, this is Matthew, Joshua's son. Can I take a message? (Pause.) Funeral?"

Matthew grabbed the pen and notepad off the fridge and wrote the information down. Luke was now in the kitchen. Matthew motioned for Luke to take Jon back up the stairs.

I was speechless. Joanna was always full of life. She had so many goals she wanted to accomplish. She didn't seem like the type to commit suicide.

I thought her new marriage was much better than ours was. He was a much better provider than I could've ever been. They came from the same upper middle class background. He wasn't as damaged and clueless about the game of marriage as I was. I was looking for a mother. He was looking for a wife.

I can't imagine what James was going through right now. They had a two-year old son together, James the III whom they called JJ and she was expecting? Oh my God. How terrible! James was in for a long road ahead.

The generational curse continues. I lost my parents, each of my older sons lost a portion of me and their mothers and now Jon had lost his mother. Jon loved spending weekends with her. She got to do all the fun stuff with Jon but I knew it tore her up not being around him more.

Was Jon and James not enough? She had struggled with depression but looking back, me being her husband likely exacerbated her pain. I thought this new marriage would have been a cure all of sorts.

I loved Joanna but James was a better match. Even I could see that. After years working in Corporate America, Joanna took James advice and became a stay-at-home wife which she fought. I didn't have enough money for her but it seems as if James may have had too much. Joanna was not the *sit still and watch the kids* type of woman. She was an awesome mother but she was a do-er.

I wonder if that was too much for her. She did grow quieter over the years. I wonder if James was as much of a match as I thought he was for her. A well-loved woman doesn't kill herself when she has a six-year-old, two-year-old and another one on the way. If Anthony Bourdain and Robin Williams could kill themselves, I guess we are all susceptible to going over the deep end. Oh Joanna, what happened? I thought to myself. I began to cry.

Just when I was looking forward to going to see Tasha every weekend! Look at me thinking of ass at a tragic time like this! I rebuked myself for being so petty.

"My first wife committed suicide. We'll have to change our schedule," I told Tasha the first chance I got. I still was unsure how to tell Jonathan about this. How do you tell a six-year old that their mother is gone?

Joanna couldn't stand me (for good reason). But her mother Grace loved me and adored Jonathan. Jonathan was her first grandson after four granddaughters by her other children. I drove over to the house.

The well-coiffed Mrs. Grace Royal's hair was a hot mess. If grief-stricken had a look, Mom Grace wore it. Ted, her new white husband, explained everything as Mom Grace went into hysterics after seeing me at the door. Joanna's father, Walter, died halfway into our short marriage. I didn't realize he was 15 years older than Grace. Her being with him aged her.

I really believe her father's passing spurred our divorce. Joanna didn't want to waste time where she was unhappy which is why her suicide a few years later didn't make sense. Why with a seemingly beautiful new marriage would she take her life?

Joanna's boss called Grace and said they hadn't heard from her in a week. Ted had a new cabin in the woods that he let Grace's family use. They thought Joanna might've gone there. She'd been going there once a month to chill especially with the baby coming. Jonathan and Joanna would go there on the weekends because it was near a creek where they would go fishing. They could bond as mother and son with privacy.

"But why would her boss call and not James?" I asked Ted. Ted was a widow too. A tall stately man. Ted was a retired police chief. He wasn't necessarily warm but he was a strong solid man. He was gentle with Grace though. He was the type of man you'd want your aging mother to have around her as the neighborhood begins to go down.

Ted tilted his head urging me to get it. There were several people around the house talking in hushed tones. Ted grabbed my arm and led me to the kitchen.

"I don't think it was a suicide," he admitted when we were by ourselves.

"When word got to James, he seemed quite unimpressed that his pregnant wife had gone missing," Ted said.

Police rely a lot on instincts. I knew that when I was in the streets. They're like human cats. If he had a hunch that James was the culprit, I'd believe him.

"I tried to tell your mom but it's just too much for her to want to admit so soon. She just can't fathom how he could even think about, let alone do something so heinous."

James went to Yale Law, every mother-in-law's dream.

"They found the body in the cabin locked with her pills displayed all around her like they had been positioned there to look like she took them. I'm still waiting on the autopsy to see what was really in her system. I told my friends on the force to watch him. I told them I do not believe this was a suicide. There is no type when it comes to suicide but Joanna adored Jon and was looking forward to having this baby. There's no way she would have killed herself. She was so excited when she found out she was having a little girl."

"Wow, this is too much for even me," I responded. "Have you tried pressing charges?"

"Yes I have," Ted said, nodding his head.

"Grace didn't want me to cause a fuss because the Rice's have more money, but when a man kills a pregnant woman he should go to jail. Jon and James don't have a mother anymore. Something like this..." He paused.

"He may have done this before. You know, his first wife died in her *sleep*," he said with air quotes.

"I'm so glad you're in our lives. Grace is gonna need you now more than ever. This is terrible," I said, shaking my head.

We heard Grace go hysterical again. "Talk to you later." Ted rushed out of the kitchen to be by her side.

It seemed every time someone came to the door, she went off. Joanna had three other siblings but Joanna was Grace's favorite because she was so smart and successful. I considered Joanna's father, Walter and Ted and it's no wonder why Joanna was disgusted with me. It's a wonder how Grace could stand me.

Walter and Ted were one of a kind and I had a lot of growing up to do when Joanna came into my life. They were quintessential husbands—good with money, a strong presence but knew when to turn it off and be gentle. I was out the streets but I didn't know the role of the husband like Walter and Ted seemed to. I watched Ted sit and hold Grace, shoo people away, bring her juice and walk her to the bathroom, all while making calls to the funeral home and the police department. He was built for times like these. Talk about a Monday from hell. James was nowhere in sight

"He's grieving with his parents and JJ," Ted said, when I asked where James was. Ted obviously didn't believe James.

"He was pushing for Joanna to be cremated but Joanna left Grace as the executor of her estate without James knowing it. She made that decision about a year ago when they had a bad fight. Grace is going to get all the life insurance except what's designated for Jon and James. He is pissed. His lawyers are chomping at the bit as we speak. Their friends of his from Yale."

"Joshua, don't let Jon out of your sight. She left a lump sum for each of them and if one dies, the other gets both lump sums. He's not grieving Joanna. He's grieving the fact that he won't get paid. That's how he bought that 3,000 sq. ft. house over there—the life insurance from the first wife."

When I got home, I sat on the bed and wept like a baby. Joanna was a bitch to me but she had so many goals to accomplish. She had already written her first book. She had a strong social media following that afforded her an even more comfortable life than her cushiony corporate job. Her followers were devastated. Somehow they found the funeral home address and were sending flowers day and night for their Joanna.

Some were asking the hard questions about James too. They had whole pages dedicated to finding out what happened to Joanna. When James tried to shut one website down, another would crop up in its place. Joanna adored Jon and James, and I'm sure she would want nothing but the best for the little girl she was carrying. James better move fast because #whathappenedtojoanna was becoming a trending hashtag. I went on YouTube and Instagram to see her final videos and posts to see if I saw any signs of sadness, any little *joke* that would suggest suicide was on the horizon. She had posted about buying girl's clothes for the first time and her new pink diaper bag custom made by a subscriber who she partnered with to advertise her baby bags. She was so excited to finally be a #girlmom.

The Worst Is Yet to Come

The funeral was one for the books. I never knew Joanna to have many friends but the church was packed. Quite a few of her followers were in the audience. Jonathan was stoic. He insisted on seeing his mother in the casket. He told her *goodbye* at the front of the church.

Mom Grace was despondent. In as little as seven days, she had aged considerably and had lost a vast amount of weight. Joanna's brother, Pat along with Ted literally carried Mom Grace to her seat. She wailed, she got quiet, she wailed and then got quiet all over again.

James was in jail while under investigation. It helps having the ex-police chief as your step-dad. Justice is served much quicker that way. Even with the Rice's money, he was taken into custody. He must've been sloppy with the evidence. Ted and I went to the police station to talk to the Rice family two days before the funeral. They seemed willing to accept some prison but not a maximum sentence. They also wanted him to go to one of the nicer prisons in the area. This nigga done killed two people that we know of, and his parents want him to be at the Holiday Inn while he does his time. Rich people!

Joanna spoke so highly of James and he genuinely seemed like a nice man. She glowed after she got rid of me. It was no wonder she got married so easily. Everything was still alleged at the time of the funeral so with their money, James was out and about and able to come to the funeral and play the sad widower role. All eyes were on him. There were about five police officers at the back of the church. I had never felt so scared at a funeral before in my life. Joanna's sister, Elaine, instructed everyone before making remarks not to make mention the way she died and just talk about her. Things were uncertain. A few people still made unique remarks.

One co-worker said, "I know she didn't commit suicide." The Pastor and Elaine damn near threw her off the stage but many people clapped.

"Amen!" Some of the congregants said.

Ted told me later that James brought in a lot of money to that church being the hotshot lawyer that he was. James and the Pastor were very close. I'm sure this had to be embarrassing for him. New, well-monied members embroiled in a murder scandal.

"She was so happy and full of life. She would spend hours at Babies R Us. She was looking forward to having her little girl. It just doesn't make sense," a neighbor said before stepping away from the microphone. People *mmm-hmmed* in agreement.

I don't remember Joanna ever being *happy* or *full of life*. Getting rid of me must've changed her for the better. That hurts to admit. Jon fell asleep through the funeral. Tasha sat next to us.

I was happy to have Tasha here. She had become my rock. This was a curveball in our courtship but Tasha was so tender with Jon. Her daughter, Kia, was Tasha 2.0. She was so sweet with Jonathan. She taught him new games. Playing with her helped keep Jonathan's mind off his Mom. At least I hoped it did.

I think Tasha saw Joanna's death as even more of an open door for us. Her being with Jonathan reinforced that he would need a mom. She didn't have to show up the way she did. I knew he needed a mom and I already knew she would be his stepmom when I saw her outside of the Charthouse, but I accepted her love as it was given. Jon knew he could cry with me but with Tasha he was so tender. He cried much more freely with her. It's amazing how children know the gifts and boundaries of each gender instinctively.

The rest of the service was loud. The family was trying to keep things positive with the *we know she was saved* and *in a better place.* Joanna was 37 and pregnant. This was no *celebration of life.* This was a funeral.

Mom Pat and Pop Pop, my paternal grandparents, took Jon back to the house after the funeral. She had stayed with us for a few days. Jon wasn't the only one grieving. I stayed with Mom Grace and Ted until the last guest left the church after the repast. You could tell this was a beautiful church family. They were so sweet to the family and the rest of the mourners. The food was good too. Mom Grace wanted to go back to the cemetery but Ted refused it.

"Tomorrow, yes. But today, you need rest. It's been a long day," Ted demanded. His son Brian and daughter Elaine were nearby to help Mom Grace put her coat on. Elaine was now the oldest child. She lost her big sister. I could only imagine what that felt like—for the birth order to be rearranged that quick.

Ok Kid. "Keep us in prayer. I going to speak with our lawyers. I think there's enough evidence to put that animal to sleep," Ted said after he got Mom Grace safely in her car before stepping around to the back.

"They found his footprints all over the cabin. She wasn't prescribed any of those meds that they found by her bed. Her urine samples were clean when she went for prenatal appointment two days prior. His girlfriend was a pharmacist and knew the best concoction for her to sleep in heavenly peace," he said before realizing that was a bad joke.

I was speechless. I got out my checkbook and wrote a check for $10,000 to help with legal fees. This was Ted's turn to cry.

"We really need this. I love this woman," he said, motioning to Grace.

"He stole the light out of her eyes. It may take years for her to bounce back. He has to pay for that too," Ted said, his voice breaking as he turned away from me. His son was standing close by, listening too. He wiped a handkerchief across his eyes.

"It's okay, Dad,'" Ted's son said. "Thank you. We appreciate this." Ted's son said to me.

"Brian, this is Josh, Joanna's first husband. Josh, this is my oldest," Ted said, introducing us.

"Your son? Who would've thought that?" I joked. Brian looked like Ted minus 30 years. It only made sense that Brian had his father's name. They both appreciated the humor.

"Brian, you take care of your dad and I'll take care of Mom Grace, okay?" I said as if assigning duties.

"Sounds good to me."

Ted took his Grace home and Brian and I finished helping the church clean up after the repast. I didn't get home until 8 pm. I had no desire to do anything but sleep.

We need to talk to you. Mary, Tasha and Chris said via a group text.

What the hell is going on? I responded.

Why is Chris on this thread? He is a co-worker. He doesn't need to know our business? I texted Mary and Tasha. I was unnerved that Tasha couldn't tell me directly.

It was about six weeks after the funeral. I was still getting over that and helping Jonathan manage. Tasha, Kia, Jon and myself were inseparable on weekends.

It was still up in the air whether James was going to jail. Even rich niggas could escape real justice. Jon had to testify about how hard it's been without his mother. I was considering adopting James so Jon and James could stay together. Despite his parents, James was easy to love and looked very much like Jon. It's been rough and Tasha knew I didn't need any more surprises. I loved Mary but Tasha was mine. We were an item. Why couldn't she tell me herself?

Chris loves you like a brother. Stop shutting him out, Mary texted me and Tasha. Chris was there when Jon testified. He had babysat when I needed a Saturday to myself. He really did blur the line between friend and co-worker.

We want you to meet someone, Mary responded. *This is why I wanted to meet you for lunch privately but you keep avoiding me.*

What?

Don't get defensive, babe. When are you free? Tasha chimed in. *I said Saturday after 2 pm. Is that cool?*

No, I'm going to California to visit Tim and Mom Ellen this weekend. I won't be back until Sunday evening. I may end up staying until Tuesday. Mom Ellen is in the hospital.

OMG! Even better! Tasha said.

Well, we'll have to do this over the phone, Mary insisted.

Mary, what the fuck do you need?

Watch it, Chris texted.

Mary called me. "Your daughter needs a blood transfusion."

The Truth of Discover

I hung up. I wasn't ready for any more news. Ever since Mary re-entered my life, my world had turned upside down.

I'm not dealing with this right now, I texted back. *Give me until I get back and we'll talk,'* I replied.

She needs a transfusion as soon as possible. She's trying to get better to not postpone her wedding, she texted. *She's at Kaiser Roseville. Since you'll be in the Bay you can just go up to Kaiser Roseville and give your blood.*

Now I was calling on the phone. Mary didn't answer. She sent me a picture of the woman she was describing a few weeks back.

This is Tiara. The girl I was asking you about several weeks ago. This is her mother.

Yes, she was several grades above me in Milton. We might've had sex. I really can't be sure. Some periods of my life I don't remember that good.

When you see her, you'll know she's yours. Your daughter looks like your Mom.

She sent me a picture of my *daughter*. She looked like my mother on the cover of her funeral program but she had touches of Tiara too.

I didn't respond for a few moments. The tears started to flow.

"Mom," I whispered. "Thank you for strong genes."

Can you help? She needs a blood transfusion. She knows I know her mother but she doesn't know that I know her father. You don't have to have a relationship just yet but if you could offer her your blood, that would help her get back on her feet,' Mary texted back. *Tiara don't even know I found you.*

I'll do it. It's the least I can do, I reply. Now I'm wondering how many other kids I may have that I don't know of. This is embarrassing.

What's her name?

Dawn. She's 24.

Birthday?

February something, I think. Tiara and I must've gotten together when I was 16 and she was 19.

Mary gave me the room number and the number of the nurse's station at Kaiser Roseville to tell them I was on my way.

You need to come ready to expect anything. Tiara is beside herself. Dawn is pretty banged up. Right now, it's about getting Tina healed. They've been looking for a B-negative blood type for a few weeks and the donors kept backing out or had bad blood. Luckily, the wedding was planned for August of the following year. Tine has 10 months to heal for the wedding. Her fiancé will be there. He is very protective of her.

I'll be there on my best behavior, I report. I was gonna need Tasha for this.

I sent the picture of Dawn to my mother's mother, Mom Ellen. Under the picture I wrote, *This is your great-granddaughter. She's in the hospital. Kaiser Roseville.*

I knew that picture let Mom Ellen know this was definitely her great-granddaughter.

What hospital? Can I come? What time? Mom Ellen didn't play when it came to family. After I had lived with the Walkers and got my Associates from Community, Mom Ellen scooped me up. Tim's parents told the Austins and Mom Ellen, I was still selling.

"You need a new start. You'll stay with them out here," she ordered.

Mom Pat told me I was going to finish at the University of Maryland and when I said I'd be interested in Optometry, she used her connections to get me into John Hopkins. Her and Pop Pop paid for everything. They had friends watch me like a hawk because they still lived in Virginia.

The wealth of my father's parents was tremendous. I didn't know regular people could be rich. I thought only celebrities could have the type of money the Austins had. My Mom's Mom really fucked up losing me to the system. I could've been farther faster if I had stayed with my dad's side of the family. They had money and connections. I wouldn't have wanted for nothing.

Pop Pop paid off the mortgage on the *family home*. They adopted two brothers when my father died to fill the void, I guess. Robert and Daniel were very accomplished. They roamed so comfortably in their manhood, their personhood. I resigned to believe I would be glued to my therapist and Klonopin for the rest of my life. I had so much to unlearn and re-learn, so much to forgive, so much baggage. I envied them but they envied me. Pop and Mom put me back on the throne when I got to Maryland. They were their sons by law but I was their blood.

I often think about what if I never crossed paths with Tim? What if I didn't look so much like my father for Tim to recognize me? What if I never registered to go to school that semester? I could still be in *the life*, dead or in prison. My story was a real miracle.

And for my daughter to be named Dawn, the beginning of a new day, and look so much like my mother I knew this was a second chance. I finally have my daughter.

Robert and Daniel played nice though and offered their connections too to keep me from selling and using. Mom Ellen was right. A change of scenery was just what the doctor ordered. I stopped using and selling. My voice got higher. My skin cleared up. My appetite stabilized. I didn't depend on sex so much. I also loved how honest East Coast people were. Not that passive-aggressive shit that bothered me about the West Coast. The East Coast was much faster but I felt at home. I was my father's son.

Thanksgiving will be at my house this year. You can meet her then, I texted back.

What if she don't want to come, especially all the way to Maryland? She from here. Mom Ellen responded.

I never thought she would reject me. None of my sons rejected me when I came into their lives. I had never gone through this with a daughter. Boys yearn for their father. I didn't know if girls did.

I guess you better come on then, I resigned. I gave her the address and time to be at the hospital. I would see Mom tomorrow.

I called Tasha. "How long have you known about this?" I was pissed. That began our first fight.

Let the Fight Begin

"Why the fuck are you here?" Tiara asked abruptly. "Mary, what is going on?"

"He's a match," Mary said. Mary and Tasha had taken an earlier flight than I had. Us and Mom Ellen managed to arrive at the hospital together though.

"I would think he is," Tiara said as if Mary was dumb. Even at 8 o'clock in the morning, Tiara was not here for that bullshit. She was in Momma Bear mode.

Mom Ellen, Tasha and I stood back waiting for Mary to smooth the way. Chris came around the corner with coffee for everyone. I did not need his white ass seeing my shit like this. I can't do nothing lately without him popping up all in my business. Turns out he flew in last night and had been waiting at the hospital for us to arrive.

Dana began to squirm. Her hospital room had a window and curtains facing the hallway. She could see her mother was upset.

"We need to get her better and Dawn needs to know her people anyway. I just ran into him. He's a different person then he was. We all are," Mary said, her voice breaking. Mary really loved people but maybe this was too much.

"This ain't the time for no family reunion," Tiara stated.

A nurse popped around the corner. "Is everything okay?"

"Yes Ma'am," Tiara said. Mary and Tiara kept fussing and all I could think about was how I must've had good taste even for a junky. All my baby mommas were pretty. Whatever else was in

Tiara's DNA was coming through strong. She was looking very mixed today as if she did actually have Indian in her family.

"Look, this is about Dawn. I'm here to help," I spoke up.

"Who the fuck asked you?" Tiara said.

"Listen, I only found out about Dawn last night. I came as soon as I heard."

"You want a fucking award?" Tiara was not the mild-mannered girl I hung out with 20 years ago. Tiara today was a fighter. I wondered what caused her to turn into this.

"Tiara," Mary and I quipped.

"Mom, who is this man?" Dawn stepped out into the hallway and spoke while still attached to a machine. Even while sick, she had a beautiful voice as if she sang.

"Don't worry baby."

"Who are these people?"

"Tell her," Mary said.

"This ain't the time for no damn surprises. It's 8 am in the morning and my daughter is trying to recover."

"I'm your father," I said. I took one of my mother's pictures out of my pocket and showed Dawn her twin—my mother. She immediately recognized herself.

"This is your great-grandmother," I said pointing to Mom Ellen. "Here's another picture of your grandmother when she was your age," I said giving her another picture of herself set in the 1980s.

She looked at us and she looked at her mother. Tiara nodded. Dawn took a deep breath and blacked out.

"Nurse!" Tasha called. "Nurse!"

"What did I tell you? She had an accident three days ago and her fiancé is considering cancelling the wedding. Now was not the time for this." Tiara was livid.

"Get them out of here," she bellowed repeatedly when security had come up to settle the commotion. Tiara had become friends with one of the security guards because clearly he took her grief personally. We were out of there in a minute flat.

"Mary, I don't want to see you ever again," Tiara yelled.

The nurse ran after us. "Stop! Stop!"

"Sir, we need the blood!" The nurse said. She ushered me back into the building to the lab away from Tiara and Dawn. The women and Chris followed me like puppies.

"Her mom may not like you but she needs you now more than ever. I'm going to take a pint now and we may need more in a few days. Can you come back on Thursday if we need it?"

"Yes," I said.

She took my name and number and said she'd have more information by tomorrow morning.

"Dawn may have had a panic attack. So now we have to support her physically and mentally. She won't be leaving here for some time," the nurse reported, after taking my blood.

"Lots of fluids these next few days," she demanded.

"What happened?" I asked.

The nurse made a look that asked if I was sure I wanted to know.

"You sure you want to know?" She finally asked what her face had already said.

"Her fiancé's other girlfriend who didn't get a proposal tried to run her off the road. That's why the wedding is up in the air," she said. The nurse enjoyed spilling this tea but tried to pretend to be professional towards the end.

"Are you kidding? No wonder Tiara was so defensive of her. They must be very close."

"You have a lot of catching up to do, Papa," the nurse said shaking her head.

Chris and the women were enraged when I told them about the real reason behind the *bad accident*. Marty was about to find the fiancé and that other girlfriend.

"Let's just give them some space," I suggested. I got Tiara's number. I would text her in a week to see how Dawn was coming along. Dawn and I had lost 24 years already. I was not going to lose any more time. Tim had come to pick Mom Ellen up but I walked with Tasha back into the billing department.

"What's Tiara's last name," I asked Tasha.

"Booker."

When my number was called, I asked the clerk, "Is Ms. Dawn Booker covered by insurance? Does she have any outstanding debts as of today? She was brought here a few days ago. So you may not see anything."

"We can't give out that information. HIPPA," the Hispanic clerk said.

"I don't need to know her condition, just if she's paid up. I'm her father," I said.

"I bet you are," she quipped.

"Can you put my card on file in case she runs up any charges?" Tasha did a double take.

"No," she said flatly.

"Okay. I guess I'll have to wait and double check with her mother when she gets released." I said to myself but out loud.

When Tasha and I got into the car, Tasha asked. "So how much money do you have?"

The Truth Comes Out

Thanksgiving had come and gone. James was still not in prison. Dawn was healed and her wedding plans were destroyed. Dawn and the girl who tried to run her over were not the only ones her fiancé' was messing with.

My daughter was open to a relationship with me but Tiara was not. She was angry that she had lost her youth raising Dawn. I created a bunch of bitter sons and middle aged women. She was jealous that I was able to bounce out of *the life* and have a real life while she was struggling to take care of Dawn. I had grandparents to fall back on. She only had herself.

Apologizing to Tiara had become our only mode of conversation. But I knew if I wanted to continue to build a relationship with Dawn, I had to do whatever Tiara said. She was gorgeous but jaded as hell. Dawn was apprehensive at first as could have been expected but more open. She at least tried. I committed to keep trying too.

Girls were definitely different. With my sons, I could invite them to a football game or to go shoot pool. Where do you start with girls? Money. Dawn grew up poor so money really helped. We Face Timed twice a week but she was a consummate texter. I tried to make it out to California at least once a quarter. Dawn spent a lot of time with Mom Ellen. Tiara was Dawn's mother but she wasn't motherly. How could she be? She had to be a dad and protect Dawn in the bowels of East Oakland.

Every now and then, I'd send Dawn enough money to pay her rent. She racked up tickets. When she mentioned she'd needed her car fixed, I put it on my card. Tiara told me a few things she liked. So off to the mall I went for gift cards. Tiara, Dawn and I would hang out together when I was in town. Dawn was a pleasant young woman. I definitely knew why any man would want to marry her so young. She already had a Master's in Education, was well spoken, very pretty and genuinely a likeable person like her grandmother. She was on track to become a principal by 30 and a superintendent by 40. How sweet Dawn came from bitter old Tiara is beyond me.

Tiara almost seemed jealous. Dawn was the sole provider, the financial helper since Dawn entered adulthood. She seemed to envy my new role in Tina's life. She didn't like that she was less needed. Tiara really put her life on hold for Dawn. I can never understand what that cost her.

"But you didn't tell me," I told her over our many arguments about Dawn.

"You didn't give me the opportunity to be a father."

"And what would you have done? Buy pampers with your drug money?"

"Yes!" I replied. "Pampers and formula would've been the least I could do."

"You were three years younger than me. That means nothing now but when you're 19, that makes a huge difference."

She was right.

"I didn't want Dawn growing up like us. So I got clean real quick and got my act together. She was not going into foster care if I could help it."

"Tiara, you did a marvelous job," I tell her again.

"Fuck you," she'd say and storm away.

God told me to keep thanking her for Dawn AND to send her money too. I did. Tasha didn't like that. So I just didn't tell her but I know she knew. Tiara deserved heaven for the quality of a daughter she raised. There were young women who were raised in middle class two parent homes that were strung out on meth.

Tiara and Dawn made the flight and came to our Thanksgiving festivities. Tasha was in rare form with all the cooking she did. I had planned to propose that night but Chris proposed to Mary—in my house. I decided to wait to not take away from their moment.

Chris and Mary had become such great friends. Our kids saw each other every day. James Jr. was now a part of my brood. He lost his mother and father. Mary and Chris' kids slept over our house with wanton abandon. I was either going to propose on Christmas or New Year's. Chris had ruined my show.

Mom, Tim's Mom, was now living with Amber down in Charlotte. It was very close to the end. We were all waiting for the final call at this point. I asked Amber if it would be okay if we had Thanksgiving over her house. They wanted a quieter Thanksgiving this year. It was almost like she was already preparing herself for the worse.

Mom Ellen was now living with me. I demanded she move in with me. Tim had proven a poor caretaker as she needed more assistance. She and Tasha clashed sometimes but they seemed to play nice most of the time. Mom Ellen helped Tasha put the stank on Thanksgiving dinner.

Ted and Mom Grace came to Thanksgiving as well. Mom Grace was still grieving. She was getting back to her old self but she was definitely changed. She told me of a few new illnesses that cropped up that I knew were stress related. Ted, however, was so proud of himself for getting James closer to a life term, despite the Rice's money. On TV, cases get closed so quickly. It could be another year before James' final trial and sentencing was complete. He was enjoying his last year as a free man.

James had confessed to the murders of both of his wives for the lesser sentence instead of the death penalty. Jonathan was completely over the loss of his mother which I think helped Mom Grace heal. She was still very active in his life. I knew it would affect him later in life but for right now his 7-year-old brain was over it.

"Congratulations," everyone beamed as Mary showed off her ring. Chris and Mary were indeed a cute couple and their kids did blend well.

It seemed that Mary had already started planning her wedding in the moments after the engagement.

"My colors will be maroon and white. We'll have an elegant fall wedding," she said. I couldn't have been more happy for the both of them. She already had her Pinterest wedding board created.

The Austins, my father's parents had come over with Robert and Daniel's families. They hung with Mom Grace and Ted. Mom Pat had beat cancer for the third time but they were noticeably slower as well. Rob and Daniel seemed to each assign themselves to one parent or the other. Robert and his white wife cared for Pop Pop. Daniel and his husband cared for Mom Pat. Pop Pop and Mom Pat secretly hated both of their in-laws. Luke who was at Hampton University, routinely checked in on his great grandparents as the Austins lived in Richmond. He didn't like the in-laws either. He barely liked Robert and Daniel.

The families loved on Dawn and Tiara. Tiara couldn't help but to get emotional. She was a part of our family now. All of my sons were there as well. I begged my son's mothers and families to let me steal them for this year's Thanksgiving. I wanted them to meet Dawn. Beg was too light of a word. I promised, if they give them to me for Thanksgiving, I won't bother them about Christmas.

Deacon Brown and his wife came over too. Their kids were all over the country and not one of them thought to come spend Thanksgiving with their parents. I thought that was sad but telling. I was thankful all my children were under my roof for Thanksgiving. Pastor Nickles had left pastoring for good and a new pastor was just appointed. His wife left him for a man who was more attentive to her and that must've broke him. I invited him to Thanksgiving but he declined the invitation. I understand. I hadn't seen him in months. I was still looking for a church home but Deacon Brown was still Dad to me.

An Interesting Twist

James, John, Dawn, Mary and Chris were visiting Tasha at her church for Family and Friends' Day. Kia, Tasha's daughter, was a little older than Jon. She was the consummate only child. She could make friends with a tree but still be very independent. She bossed the boys around like they were her kids. She would make the perfect big sister for them.

Tasha was surprised that all of us had made the trip from Maryland to see her. Dawn flew in and we knew she and Tiara would visit us more and more. Tiara didn't have any family so we adopted her. I was working with Dawn to get a job on this coast so she could be with us. She was considering a few offers from some private schools. She had done a few Skype interviews so it was only a matter of time before she would get a job offer.

Tiara, like my sons, had a lot of healing to do. Us Face Timing was not enough. She was too smart to pick the losers she did so I knew it had to do with me.

I knew if Dawn came, Tiara would come too. Tiara was Dawn's shadow and had centered her life around her. She didn't have any friends, boyfriends, lovers, church family, nothing. Like Nicole, Luke's mom, she clung to her child. That had to be both assuring but stifling to Dawn.

I had offered to pay for Tiara to go traveling with a few women's online travel groups. She deserved a vacation but she wouldn't go unless Dawn was interested. Dawn wasn't interested in traveling with a bunch of middle aged women. One time, Dawn wanted to go to Vegas with her friends. I told Tiara I was paying for the trip and she wasn't invited. Tiara cussed me out. She called Tasha and cussed her out too. Eventually Dawn paid for her mother to join them. Somehow, Tiara didn't want to see what was about to go down and made other plans.

When we arrived at church, Pastor Pickens was preaching about Jacob and Rachel. At 69, he was 6'6. His daughter said he had shrunken as he got older. He intimidated me at 6'6 so I could only imagine him at his full height of 7'1.

He was the perfect man to have all girls. Jon and James stayed out of his way. If God had a face, it was Pastor Pickens with his black skin, head full of white hair and a full smile. He must've been something in his day. He maintained a mid-size church. He knew me and Tasha were an item.

When he first found out we were dating, he did a full investigation on me. He called my ophthalmology practice to make sure I was employed. One Sunday after church when he knew I would be visiting, he pulled Tasha and I into his office. His daughter Sheryl, the church secretary, shut the door and gave me the worst look ever.

"I want to show you something," he said to Tasha.

He gave her copies of my juvie records. He told her I had an outstanding child support balance for Luke (three years AFTER Luke had turned 18) that had just been paid off. He showed her that I had owed Joanna, my ex-wife alimony but she passed before I paid her. He had pulled my credit reports.

"Jon is not his only child," he went on. He told her I had four older children and rattled off their names.

"Five children that the courts know of," he said, looking at me. I was floored.

"His name may not really be Joshua," Pastor Pickens said. He was on a roll.

"I didn't find any medical records that would give me pause but I would demand one immediately if you even want to continue seeing this *Joshua*," he said with air quotes.

Pastor Pickens said he always wanted to be a lawyer. He came up in a time when the smartest thing a Black man could become was a preacher. The way he pulled out one damning piece of evidence after another against me like he was in a courtroom, I knew he would've been an excellent lawyer.

"Mothafucka, you got some nerve!" I said.

"If you do anything to my daughter," pointing to Tasha, "I will knock your head off!" He barked back.

His daughter Sheryl restrained him for my sake. He opened a bottom drawer to grab something like he was ready for more than a verbal confrontation.

"Daddy, no!" Sheryl said. Pastor Pickens was saved but he was from North Philadelphia.

"Jay! Pastor, I grew up with him. I know his background. We've both been through a lot in our lives. He's a changed man. He knows all his kids and all his kids know him and adore him."

I left that office fuming. Tasha didn't have a father but Pastor Pickens filled that role perfectly today. Tasha had only been at his church for a year but he was not about this member being gobbled up by some nigga. I hated him and wanted to be him all at the same time.

I tried to get Tasha to leave his church. Tasha was a lay member up until that point. After that, Tasha lived at that church. She baked him cakes, pies, everything. Pastor gained another daughter.

"He did what he was supposed to do," Deacon Brown told me when I recounted the story. I knew he was right.

Another year passed. Pastor Pickens and I were cordial but I was still humiliated by what he did.

But on one particular day my mind was full of emotions. I couldn't believe Pastor Pickens had said yes to offer.

Just before the benediction he said, "We have one more announcement."

Dawn got up and took the mic. I got up to get in position.

"Falling in Love with Jesus," Dawn belted out softly.

"Tasha, can you come forward?" I asked. She walked up to the front of the sanctuary reluctantly. Tasha had gotten so shy over the years. Chris, who slept through most of the sermon, was now wide awake.

"You are the best thing that ever happened to me," I said. I pulled a small black box out of my pocket. I got down on one knee.

The women squealed. Tasha melted.

"Go 'head girl," Sister Gallashaw said. "Go get yo' man."

"Tasha, will you marry me?"

"Absolutely," Tasha replied. "I love this ring." Two thumbs up for Joshua.

Chris was recording. I later found out that Pastor Pickens even shed a few tears.

I was in the Groom's suite nervous as hell, drinking the wine offered to us by the hotel. Chris, Brian, Robert, Daniel and Marc were getting ready.

The day was finally here. Jonathan, now almost nine, was my ring bearer. He squirmed in his suit but he was clean as a whistle. He looked more and more like his mother every day. *Thank you God,* I whispered.

The year, this day, had been full of preparation and nervousness. All our hard work and planning had come down to this. Tasha was in rare form planning this ordeal. I was fine going to the courthouse but she refused. I wanted a small gathering but she said, *Hell no. I've been waiting my whole life for this.*

It was New Year's Day and I was about to start my new life. The wedding planner poked her head in and said, "It's time."

Pastor Pickens was in position at the altar in his purple and gold regalia. He had conducted our marriage counseling. I have to admit that his counseling was much more thorough than the counseling I got for my first marriage.

He shook my hand. Classical music was playing. Mom Ellen and Mom Pat were already in tears when I got into position. They didn't like Joanna but they tolerated her because of me. This time, they loved Tasha more than they loved me. That's how I knew Tasha was the one.

Mom Ellen and Mom Pat were so much alike. I definitely understood how their offspring, my parents, were so compatible. Mom Grace and Ted sat a few rows back. It was nice to have their blessings too. Mom Grace had shaken off the grave clothes of grief and the light in her eyes had returned.

Dawn began singing *Falling in Love with Jesus* by Jonathan Butler. The whole room melted. All I saw were women dabbing their eyes.

The bridesmaids came down one by one to a Prince song. Mary was the matron of honor. Kia, Nicole and Princess, Tasha and Mary's daughters, were the flower girls. They had those dresses with the petals in the bottom part. They were so cute.

Tim and three members of the church were our runners. Tim's mother had died last spring. Tim's sisters, Vanessa and Amber, and their families were here. Both daughters were now with new husbands. I was glad. Dan was too white washed and Dante was zesty, if you know what I mean. When Amber told me the last straw was finding gay porn on his computer, I was not surprised. She was upset that I, nor anyone else in her family, was surprised by that news.

"Why didn't you say something?" She asked. None of us had the heart to tell her that it was obvious that there was really nothing for us to say. But the *last straw* was what I was angry about.

By the time she got finished running down the *last straw* list, I had my nine millimeter in my hand ready to go find Daniel. Amber and Vanessa begged me to chill. Of course, their actual brother could care less. I could've killed him too, his ol' useless ass.

I still sent some goons to pay Daniel a visit. I told them to not kill him but just scare him. Best $5,000 I ever spent. I told Ted so he could keep his cop friends away. Ted was old school. Some men needed jail, like James. Others just needed a good ass whoopin'. Word got around to Robert and he had oh so conveniently took a job in Japan to avoid his whoopin.'

I went from having no family to four Mothers—Pat, Ellen, Grace and Bev—and four Dads—Rev. Walker, Pop Pop, Ted and Deacon Brown. Four Brothers—Chris, Tim, Robert, and Daniel—and three Sisters—Mary, Amber and Vanessa. Five boys, a daughter and now granddaughter. Marc and Dana had a little girl and were engaged to be married later in the year.

"You did it backwards," I told Marc.

"You have a nerve," Marc quipped. He was right. That was the end of that.

I waved at Pastor Nickles in the audience. He had a new woman sitting next to him, much prettier and younger than the former First Lady. She didn't sit close to him like a girlfriend so I assumed this woman may have been his daughter. Pastor did not look well.

The white runner was rolled down the aisle. I now needed a tissue.

"All Rise," Pastor Pickens said. The doors opened.

The woman of my dreams who I had known all my life, was standing at the back of the church. She would become Mrs. Brian Austin, III. All I knew was I was in the perfect place at the perfect time waiting on the perfect woman with His light and glory shining on us.

Sometimes, dreams do come true.

www.ingramcontent.com/pod-product-compliance
Lightning Source LLC
Chambersburg PA
CBHW071823190726
48292CB00005B/1577